Linda Albert's Advice for COPING WITH KIDS

Linda Albert's Advice for COPING WITH KIDS

Linda Albert

E. P. DUTTON INC.   NEW YORK

Published in the United States by E. P. Dutton, Inc.
2 Park Avenue, New York, N.Y. 10016

Library of Congress Cataloging in Publication Data

Albert, Linda.
    Linda Albert's Advice for coping with kids.

    1. Child rearing.   I. Title.   II. Title: Advice for coping with kids.
HQ769.A359   1982   649'.1   82-2524
                                         AACR2

ISBN: O-525-93262-3

Published simultaneously in Canada by Clarke, Irwin & Company Limited, Toronto and Vancouver

10 9 8 7 6 5 4 3 2 1

First Edition

To my children,

KEN

JUDY

STEVE

who survived the early years before
    I learned to cope with kids,

who, willingly or not, experienced the changes
    as I learned new parenting skills and techniques,

who encouraged and supported my efforts
    to share these ideas with other parents,

and who have now become loving, self-directed,
    self-confident, responsible young adults.

Contents

Acknowledgments

I have been able to write *Linda Albert's Advice for Coping with Kids* because of the help and encouragement I have received from many people.

I was not fortunate enough to ever meet either Dr. Alfred Adler or Dr. Rudolf Dreikurs while they lived. Yet it is their legacy of information about children that forms the theoretical foundation for the advice given in this book.

The original work of Adler and Dreikurs has been developed and expanded by many of their followers throughout the world. My own understanding of children and parents was deepened by my association with these people, their writings, and their presentations at meetings and conventions sponsored by the North American Society of Adlerian Psychology. To these people, most of whom I do not know personally, I say Thank you. To those whom I do know personally, in particular Dr. Oscar Christensen, Dr. Sylvia Cowan-Anderson, Dr. Marie Hartwell-Walker, Dr. Maxine Ijams, and Dr. William Marchant, a very special thanks for your friendship and help as I endeavored to learn and apply these principles of raising children.

To the people of the *Ithaca Journal* and the Gannett News Service in Washington, who supported me in the transition from speaker to writer, including Alvin Greene, Marilyn Greene, Terry Hopkins, Joe Junod, Jerry Langdon, and Tamar Sherman, thanks.

To the many readers of the "Coping with Kids" newspaper columns, who contributed the questions which appear in this book, thanks,

To Ann DuBois, Rick Brandon, and Ed Lisbe, who gave their time and talent in reading the original manuscript and offering suggestions, thanks,

To my agent Jeanne Drewsen, whose excitement about this manuscript encouraged me to persevere and finish the project, thanks,

To Diane Harris, senior editor at Dutton, whose many fine insights and suggestions are incorporated into this book, thanks,

To Wilbur Young, friend and companion, who gave me encouragement and moral support when needed, thanks,

And last, but perhaps most important of all, to the one person who has edited every word I have ever written, and offered invaluable suggestions, advice and encouragement, my daughter Judith M. Rachel, many many thanks from a very grateful mother.

Linda Albert's Advice for COPING WITH KIDS

Note to Readers

Our language lacks a satisfactory pronoun that can refer to either a boy or girl. The masculine pronoun used throughout this book applies to children of both sexes.

1

•••••••••••••••••••••••••••••••••••••••

The Parenting
Dilemma

Parents frequently ask me why it's so difficult to raise kids today. Before their first child was born, most prospective parents felt confident about their abilities to raise children effectively. A few years later these same parents are often confused and discouraged. Their children and the problems they cause are a source of distress instead of pleasure. "Where did we go wrong?" they ask. "Why do our kids cause so many problems? Why can't we succeed like everybody else?"

The truth is that everyone else is not succeeding. The pages of this book contain dozens of questions from parents encountering problems in raising their children. These questions show that the concerns and difficulties so many parents face are normal or at least commonplace. No one experiencing difficulties raising children is in a unique position.

How can we account for the widespread existence of so many problems in raising children today?

Each of us has a tool kit of parenting skills and techniques which we use to raise our children. Most of these are derived from observing others. Our first source is usually what we learned as children in our families; the skills and techniques our parents used on us. Because we experienced the effects of such tools firsthand, when we are faced with a situation involving our own kids we often use similar skills and techniques. Occasionally we may have a strong dislike for some of the methods our parents used, and we make conscious decisions not to repeat these. Our second source is methods we learned from others back in our childhood, from aunts and uncles or neighbors.

The dilemma of today's parent is that many of these skills are ineffective with kids growing up in the 1980s. Yet we hate to discard them or even admit that they don't work. After all, our parents raised us by using these techniques, and we turned out okay. So, instead of discarding them, we use the same ones over and over and over again, only to find that they don't work the second time, or the third, or the fourth.

The only thing parents can do to get out of this dilemma is to replace ineffective tools with more effective ones. To find new strategies, parents often ask relatives or friends who have kids how to handle certain situations. Or they may have informal get-togethers at which they share and discuss specific problems. Still others join parent study groups, organized by schools, churches, or family service organizations, where they learn new skills from formal courses of study. Perhaps most often people seek to replenish their skills by availing themselves of printed information on parenting. The goal of this book is to offer a wide variety of effective techniques, which the many parents with whom the author has worked have used successfully.

You will notice that the skills presented here are action-oriented. When it comes to coping with kids, actions speak much louder than words. What parent hasn't tried asking, yelling, threatening, reminding, criticizing, and nagging, all with very few positive results? Children learn very early to become parent-deaf, to act as if our words weren't spoken. Our actions in response to the kids' misbehavior influence them to behave in a different manner, not our words.

Many parents discourage themselves by dwelling on past errors in parenting. They frequently say to themselves "If only I had been more patient," or "If only I had handled toilet training differently," or "If only I had known how to stop the fighting." Well, the past is past, gone, unchangeable. And while it might have been desirable not to have made the mistakes you made, few mistakes are so terrible that they will leave indelible scars on your child. So don't waste your energy regretting past mistakes. Instead, learn to use the effective parenting tools described in detail in the following chapters.

A word of warning. Most children are not too pleased when parents begin to change their parenting style because, believe it or not, the kids have us well trained. They usually know just how to manipulate us to get their own way and therefore they are quite comfortable with the way things are.

So be prepared. You may follow all the hints in this book, choose an appropriate situation, apply your new parenting tools correctly, and all of a sudden your child's behavior gets worse. Don't despair. It is not necessarily a sign that the behavior is not correctable or that you have failed, or that the advice in this book is worthless. As you learn new parenting skills, and the kids begin to realize that they will no longer be able to manipulate you so easily, they often increase the intensity of their misbehavior and their manipulations in an attempt to force you to revert to your old parenting style.

Thus, when you follow the advice offered here, and the behavior suddenly gets worse, it may be a sign that you are actually succeeding! Improvement in your children's behavior will come as soon as they are convinced that the changes you are making are permanent.

Occasionally some children use very angry or even ugly, hurtful statements when they perceive that their parents are standing firm and can no longer be manipulated. It is not unusual to hear a child exclaim, "You're the meanest mom (dad) on the block," or "I'm so miserable I wish I'd never been born." Realize that these statements do not reflect the child's true feelings. They are the child's final card in a power play, a last desperate attempt to get the parent to change his or her mind and give in.

When the endless daily battles with the kids begin to subside, when the new parenting tools are used easily and effectively, parents will then experience the joys of parenthood more frequently, joys many parents have abandoned hope of ever knowing. There will be time and energy to enjoy the children, to share their joys and sorrows, to lovingly watch them grow and develop.

Children whose parents cope with them effectively are in luck, for the type of adults the children become is directly related to how they were parented. Parents who use ineffective tools, who barely cope, who do not know how to win cooperation and teach responsibility, tend to rear children who are manipulative, self-centered, and dependent. It is not easy for such children, when grown, to succeed in the adult world. When parents discard their ineffective tools, and have the courage to use the techniques recommended here, there is a much greater chance of rearing children who possess a high level of confidence and self-esteem, who are sensitive to the needs of others, and who are capable and willing to take their places in the world as responsible adults. So keep in mind the long-term goal of raising mature adults, and the short-term effort of learning to cope more effectively will seem like a small price to pay for so great a reward.

Young children, of course, can't be expected to comprehend the long-term benefits of effective parenting. Getting what they want right now is much more important to them, whether what they want is a piece of candy, getting out of a disliked chore, or conning Mom or Dad into doing something they could just as easily do for themselves. It isn't until many,

many years later, perhaps when they have children of their own, that they will realize how lucky they were to have parents who cared enough, and persisted enough, to cope effectively with their children.

This book has been written for parents who want to increase the range and usefulness of their skills. My hope is that you will refer to it frequently, much as you would a book of favorite recipes. Reread the questions and answers and reuse your favorite tools whenever you feel they would be appropriate. As you put the suggested techniques into practice in your own family and begin to apply them to a wider and wider variety of situations, you will notice how much easier it becomes to cope with your kids.

2

. . . .

Helpful
Hints

You want to cope more effectively with your children. You're tired of the repeated hassles, the constant bickering, the neglected chores, the messy rooms. You've seen some families that seem to get along pretty harmoniously. How do you achieve greater harmony in your own family? Probably you've flipped through some of the pages of this book and have already read a question or two that describes scenes similar to those you've experienced. You're anxious to try some suggestions and to see what happens.

The purpose of this chapter is to slow you down a bit. It contains helpful hints concerning your own behavior as a parent which will make you more effective in applying the advice in the chapters that follow.

Solve One Problem at a Time

Choose one situation and one set of techniques to work on at a time. This increases your ability to work consistently on a problem until it is solved. Your children probably have more than one misbehavior that you want to change, but if you tackle more than one problem at a time you will divide your concentration and energies. As you will see, there are only four basic motivations for misbehavior, and your approaches to solving different problems based on the same motivation will be similar. When you learn to handle a situation stemming from your child's desire to be boss, for example, you may see a decrease in other misbehaviors that stem from the same motivation without any direct effort on your part to initiate a change. This happens because the parent/child dynamic is the same for all boss behavior, even though the situations in which the behaviors occur may change. Also, as you learn to handle successfully one boss behavior situation, you will be perfecting tools you can use in other such situations. You'll feel more success if you don't overwhelm yourself by trying to change everything at once.

Don't Choose the Hardest Problem First

If you were just learning to use woodworking tools, you would choose a simple project to start. You would not begin by making a difficult, fancy piece of furniture. If you just had your first boxing lesson, you wouldn't jump into the ring with Mohammed Ali. The same principle holds true for parenting tools. It takes a while to become adept at using these new tools, so don't start by tackling your most difficult family problem first. Allow yourself to experience some initial success by beginning with smaller, less serious problems. Each small success not only encourages you but also encourages your children. They too will experience pleasant changes in the parent/child relationship and in the atmosphere at home as the amount of family strife lessens. These early successes will show your kids that change is a positive experience, not something to be feared.

Regressions Don't feel confused and upset if occasionally your child slips backward into a stage of behavior you thought he or she was beyond. These backward steps are part of the normal progression of development, which rarely moves steadily ahead. Accept occasional regressions as part of the normal process of growing up. Don't ridicule or scold your child for these regressions, but don't give extra attention to these behaviors, either. Realize that when regressions occur, they typically signify a period of stress for the child and that in stressful times it is love, support, and encouragement that are needed.

Expect Improvement—Not Perfection

Learn to pat yourself on the back for each small bit of improvement you see in your child's behavior that results from your use of these new tools. If you expect perfection, a complete change in behavior unaccompanied by an occasional regression to former misbehavior, you will be mighty disappointed. The path to success is not a straight line. If your child was throwing four temper tantrums a day and now is down to three, take heart! That's improvement! Keep at it and you can get the number down to two, then one, then finally no temper tantrums at all. But even then, occasionally, your child might decide to have another tantrum just to keep you on your toes.

Keep in mind that problems only seem insurmountable when you have no solution. When the old misbehavior does occur, just reuse the technique that originally solved the problem.

The more you allow yourself to enjoy every speck of improvement, the more encouraged you will feel to continue learning new ways to cope effectively with your kids. You might even keep a journal in which you write down each success as it occurs. Such a journal will be your proof of progress in becoming a more effective parent.

Avoiding the Game of "Yes, but"

In his bestselling book, *Games People Play*, the late Dr. Eric Berne described a technique or game called "Yes, but" which people often use to resist change. The quickest way to describe the game (which can be played by both parents and children) is as follows: Person A has a problem and goes to Person B for advice. B offers one or more suggestions, but A finds excuses not to take the advice. Thus, A stays stuck with the original problem. All of us at times are tempted to play this game because we think our problems are different from or worse than other people's—and because we may find it easier to stay stuck than to actually try some new skills.

To make the most of the suggestions offered here, it's important to give the new techniques a chance. So, before you reject any suggestions as too time-consuming, too difficult, or too different from the old ways, give them a fair trial. It may be that some of these will work better than others to help solve your particular problems, but all of them have been found effective by other parents who have used them. If you follow the suggestions carefully, keeping in mind the helpful hints provided in this chapter, there's every reason to believe that these parenting techniques will work for you, too.

Expect Occasional Unhappiness

No human being, man or woman, adult or child, can avoid the ups and downs of life. We do our children a disservice when we try to shield them too much from the down side of life, from the occasional unhappy experiences everyone has to confront. It's natural for parents to want their children to be happy. Yet if we rush in to try to fix things every time something goes wrong for our children, they do not learn how to deal with frustrations and disappointments that they will inevitably face when they are older. Remember, it's the small, unhappy experiences that teach a child valuable skills for coping with life's larger frustrations. Thus, it is better if we teach them to expect the bad along with the good and encourage them to learn to handle all situations as a part of life. What is self-confidence but the knowledge that one can handle whatever comes along?

But don't expect your child to have the wisdom and maturity to understand the growth that comes from dealing with occasional unhappiness. It's much more likely that children will cry or complain, perhaps throw a tantrum, or play a "pitiful me" game that is designed to get you feeling so sorry for them that you will find a way to make things better. Don't. This is the time to encourage your child to stick with it and endure the temporary unhappiness. Watch his self-confidence bloom when the situation is over and he realizes that he has the ability to handle life's less happy moments.

Don't Look to the Past to Understand Your Child's Behavior

When our children behave in ways that displease us, we often search back in time for the explanation, possibly for some parenting mistake we made or some failure on our part to meet their needs. Following the dictates of Freud and his disciples we tend to look for a traumatic past experience that has given rise to today's problem.

This is not a very useful approach. First, it is almost impossible to identify, out of all the things that have happened to a child, the "one" event that caused the problem. Even if we did identify such an event, we would be powerless to change it. In addition, the level of guilt that parents experience when they feel that somehow they are the cause of all of their children's problems often keeps parents from taking appropriate disciplinary action. Instead of discipline, they offer the child nurturing in the form of support and understanding, both of which are important at other times, but which will not be appropriate to deal with misbehavior. If you choose your parenting tools on the assumption that behavior is caused by past experiences

Don't Ask "Why" When you confront a child about a mis-behavior don't ask the question, "Why did you do it?" Ask instead, "What are your plans so this doesn't happen again?" When you ask "why" you focus on past behavior and will probably get a defensive reply as the child tries to protect him or herself from blame. When you ask, "What are your plans?" you focus on future behavior, where no blame is involved so no defenses are needed. Focusing on future leads more directly to the same goal as that of the confrontation—an assurance that the behavior will not be repeated.

you will often find yourself doing a lot of nurturing but precious little disciplining.

The Freudian approach assumes that the child has very little control over his behavior, that behavior is the result of external events which cause the child to act in certain ways.

It is much more useful to take the approach first developed by Dr. Alfred Adler and ask, "What is the purpose of the misbehavior?" This approach assumes that children misbehave by choice rather than by the uncontrollable force of past experiences. These choices are based on decisions the child makes about how to get along in the world. Yes, the child's decisions are influenced by the people and events around him, but ultimately the child makes his own choices. As a parent, you can teach your child to make appropriate choices by your response to his misbehavior.

Before you respond to a given misbehavior, it is helpful to understand the purpose behind the behavior. While children have literally dozens of misbehaviors they can choose to use, most of these behaviors are prompted by one of four motives.*

*These four motives were originally described by Dr. Rudolf Dreikurs, and are discussed at greater length in his book *Children: The Challenge,* E. P. Dutton, Inc., 1964.

Recognize the Four Basic Motivations for Misbehavior

The first motivation for misbehavior is a desire for more attention. The child who misbehaves by using an attention-getting mechanism is seeking undue attention. He not only wants to be noticed and appreciated, he wants his parents to be involved with him to an inappropriate extent. The second motivation for misbehavior is a desire for power. The child is attempting to prove that he is in control, to show the parent that he is the boss, and that no one can *make* him do anything. The third motivation is a desire for revenge. The child wants to hurt the parent in order to get even for something, usually a perceived injustice. The fourth motivation is a desire to avoid failure. The child attempts to get the parent to leave him alone by appearing helpless, disabled, incapable of doing a task adequately. When he is left alone, the child can avoid trying and thus avoid risking failure.

Notice that some of these motivations can lead to passive misbehavior. It's fairly easy to recognize the active misbehaviors—they cause disruption right under your nose and you are usually forced to deal with them at once. The passive misbehaviors are more subtle. Look at how much extra attention a kid can get by being slow, by eating one pea at a time, by being unable to find something, or by being unable to do a simple task.

Notice also that kids use lots of different misbehaviors to prove that they are the boss, that they are more powerful than their parents, that they cannot be forced to do things. The passive forms of these behaviors are often given labels that make the misbehavior seem like an inherent trait rather than a behavior that kids can use to show their power. A child who displays these behaviors is often called lazy, immature, distractable, unmotivated, underachieving, or procrastinating—or the child is said to have a "short attention span." If you look closely at a child who uses such tactics, you will often notice one mighty important contradiction. The child doesn't seem to display any of these traits when he is doing something he likes, that *he* has *chosen* to do. The traits and behaviors mysteriously appear only when someone else asks him to do something, particularly if that someone is a parent or a teacher. Don't be fooled by the relative passivity of this type of power struggle. It is no different from an active power struggle during which the child loudly and angrily refuses to cooperate.

Learn to Differentiate Between the Four Basic Motivations for Misbehavior

There are two ways to identify what motivates a particular misbehavior. The first way is for the parent to be aware of his or her own gut feelings at the moment the misbehavior occurs.

If the misbehavior is meant to get attention, the parent will feel mildly annoyed or irritated. If the misbehavior is a struggle for power, the parent will experience the much stronger feelings of anger and frustration. If the misbehavior is for revenge, the parent will feel hurt and disappointment in addition to anger and frustration. If the misbehavior is to avoid failure, the parent will feel inadequate, helpless, and defeated.

The second way to determine the category of the child's misbehavior is to watch what happens when you try to correct the misbehavior. If the motivation is attention, the child will stop the behavior temporarily when corrected. If the motivation is power, the child will continue the behavior a bit longer and will usually protest your corrective action. If the motivation is revenge, the behavior will not only continue, but will intensify before it stops. If the motivation is to avoid failure, the child will simply continue the same behavior.

It is important to differentiate between these motivations for misbehavior because different corrective techniques are needed to work effectively with different motives. Using the above guidelines, observe your children closely for the next week and practice identifying the different motivations for their misbehavior. Be aware that the most frequent mistake parents make in determining motivation is calling all misbehavior a bid for attention and not recognizing the power struggles as they occur.

Sidestep the Power Struggles

When kids engage in either the active or the passive variety of power or boss behaviors described in the last two sections of this chapter, it's all too easy for parents to respond with power or boss behavior of their own. After all, we think, we're the parents, we're supposed to be in charge. Therefore we'd better assert our authority and make the kids do what we say.

When parents engage in boss behavior, the situation usually gets worse. When parents command and demand and give orders, the confrontation with the kids gets louder and angrier. The kids become more stubborn and rebellious in their determination to show us they can't be bossed around. Even if they are overpowered and forced to give in, they'll retaliate and get even at a later time by engaging in some behavior that they know will anger us.

Parental boss behavior was once an effective tool for bringing kids into line. Most of us, when children, did what we were told when we were told. The only explanation we needed was a strong "because I told you to" from either Mom or Dad. I wish I could say parental boss behavior still is effective. It it were, there wouldn't be parents sending me questions about problems with their children, and there wouldn't be parents buying books of advice for coping with kids. Their original tool box of parenting skills would be sufficient to meet their needs.

Parents often fear that the alternative to boss behaviors is to be permissive and to allow the kids to do anything they want, to allow the kids to get away with murder. Nothing could be further from the truth. The alternatives to boss behaviors are simply more effective means to help kids learn to behave

Family Fun Time Every family needs a time during the week set aside for having fun together. When the whole family plans an activity for this time, it will be eagerly awaited by all. Do not let misbehavior during the week affect this time—there are more effective ways to handle behavior problems. Be sure that the activities planned can be enjoyed by all members of the family, regardless of age or ability.

appropriately, to behave in ways that contribute to the harmony of family life. The next four sections of this chapter, Learn the Language of Respect, When Silence Is Golden, Avoid Using Rewards and Punishments, and Share the Strategy, describe ways of influencing your children without using boss behavior and without getting into the power struggles that boss behavior brings about. As you read chapters 3 through 12, you'll find many other skills and techniques for sidestepping power struggles.

These behaviors that help you avoid power struggles have a wonderful side effect, too. From them children learn to internalize appropriate behavior, to become self-disciplined. They learn to do things not because of demands or commands, but simply because that is the way things need to be, that is the way the family can live in harmony together. They will be learning to think before they act, to anticipate the consequences of their behavior. They will be on their way to becoming mature, responsible adults.

Learn the Language of Respect

Child psychologists have often advised parents to talk to their children as they would talk to their best friends. I agree. I call the language parents need to use with children the language of respect. It is probably the most important skill for parents to master. All of the advice in this book is based on parents using this language of respect. Specific answers to questions throughout the book give concrete examples of how to speak to children when solving a variety of difficulties.

Before parents can use the right language with their chil dren, they will have to recognize and get rid of the disrespectful words most of us have in our everyday vocabularies. Throw away the words that you would find insulting, humiliating, and sarcastic if someone used them in speaking to you. Children will also be hurt by them. Throw away the commands, the demands, the direct orders. Children rebel when they hear them. Throw away the shouts, yells, and screams. Children become parent-deaf after hearing them for a while.

Use instead words that are encouraging, supportive, and uncritical. These are words that build up a kid's spirit rather than tear it down. Use words that build self-confidence and self-esteem.

The language of respect *invites* children to behave appropriately and *allows* them to enjoy the privilege of doing what needs to be done. This language reflects the attitude of respect that allows children to participate in making decisions that affect them and the entire family, and offers them appropriate choices based on their age and capabilities.

Instead of yelling and screaming, parents can learn to talk calmly and softly. They can use a pleasant tone of voice, and state consequences in a matter-of-fact manner. There is no need for the anger and hostility that so often characterizes parent-child confrontations.

Give yourself time to learn the language of respect. Most of us learned the disrespectful words a long time ago when we were little and, no doubt, like most parents, you have been using them with your children for a long time. As you apply the new skills offered in this book and you see your problems start to diminish, you'll find it easier and easier to talk to kids respectfully. Remember, expect improvement, not perfection—from yourself as well as your children.

When Silence Is Golden

Parents who are learning to avoid unpleasant confrontations and to apply consequences to misbehavior will have the greatest success when they remember the old adage: Silence is golden. Who hasn't had the experience of regretting something said in the heat of anger? Words spoken during conflicts and confrontations, which we hope will make our children more reasonable, usually just strengthen their will to resist our efforts.

Since articles and books on parenting tell us that we must learn to talk to our children, to communicate with them, we may think that times of disciplining are times to talk. But while the advice to learn to communicate is excellent, it is valid for all times *except* when a child is misbehaving. Most instances of misbehavior require action, not words. Save your words for times when things are going smoothly.

It is also important to remember the silence-is-golden rule after a child has experienced an unpleasant consequence. Postmortem lectures, I-told-you-so's, and see-what-happens-when-you-don't-listen-to-me's destroy the lesson you hope your child will learn.

And be aware that it is possible to scream with your mouth closed. Stares, frowns, pursed lips, pointing fingers can all give the same messages that words do. You can stir rebellion and resistance by looks as well as comments. Allow the consequence to be the communication.

Avoid Using Rewards and Punishments

The use of a reward and punishment system is often recommended to parents as a means for achieving effective discipline. In such a system, parents reward their children when they behave appropriately and punish them when they behave inappropriately. The specific structure of the recommended reward and punishment system ranges from very simple to very complex. No such system will be recommended in this book. For a very good reason.

The critical choice is between short-term and long-term results. You must decide whether you want to keep putting out firoo or ohongo tho bohaviur for guudi a clowor proooco. Thoro is no doubt that rewards can work if you look only at the immediate effect. Children are not dumb. If I offer my daughter 50¢ for doing the dishes tonight, she most likely will do the dishes and take my money. However, when tomorrow night rolls around and the dishes need to be done, she will probably say, "How much is it worth to you tonight for me to do the dishes?" The problem with rewards is that kids learn to expect them and demand them as their due. They often develop a What's in it for me? or a Gimme attitude. They are willing to contribute to family life only when they are rewarded for doing so.

Punishment will also work on a short-term basis. By using physical force or by withholding something important that the child wants, a parent can probably change a given behavior, but the use of punishment also has an unpleasant side effect. Whether we like it or not, children today operate on the belief that they have the same rights as their parents. They feel that if parents can punish them, they have the right to punish the parents in return. Children have many ways to punish parents. They can refuse to get along with siblings or peers. They can "forget" important family responsibilities; they can do poorly in school; they can drink or take drugs, and so on. Children learn early that a very effective way to punish parents is to adopt a behavior that goes against a cherished value of a parent. There is another unfortunate side effect of punishment. Sometimes children learn not to change the behavior that is disturbing the parents, but to concentrate instead on not getting caught. The kids learn how to be sneaky and how to lie effectively.

This book is filled with ideas for disciplining your children which will be more effective in the long run than the use of rewards and punishments.

Humiliation Humiliating a child is one of the least effective parenting tools. True, by making fun of a child you might be able to change or stop a misbehavior for the moment. But sooner or later the child will strike back at you in revenge, especially if you humiliate him in front of his peers. The short-term change in the child's behavior is not worth the long-term buildup of hostility.

Share the Strategy

Changes in your strategies for coping with kids should not be sprung on the kids as a surprise. In fact, you will be more effective in bringing about positive change in the kids' behavior if they know in advance how you are going to handle certain situations. Unexpected changes have an I-got-ya-now quality to them and are often seen by the kids as a pointless display of parental power. Children often react to such situations with a decision, not necessarily conscious, to get even with their parents at a later time. They get even by intensifying the same misbehavior or by switching to a different misbehavior that annoys their parents even more.

When you have identified a situation to work on, you can read or discuss with your kids the appropriate questions and answers in this book. By doing so, you sidestep this desire to get even. The kids must see that it is not your need for parental power or a desire to hurt them that accounts for the changes you make. It's simply that you find certain situations disturb the harmony of family life, and this book shows methods you can use to remedy these situations.

Remember, any suggestion I give is only one of the many possibilities for handling a given situation. Use this book as a springboard for family discussions and see if your kids come up with solutions that they feel would be more effective. Listen carefully to their ideas, for when they suggest and agree to solutions they will have a lot more motivation toward making those solutions work.

Don't Give Up if Mom and Dad Don't Agree

When parents don't achieve the ideal of complete agreement on parenting techniques, they often experience feelings of frustration and helplessness. While it certainly makes life easier for everyone concerned when parents are in agreement, parents who disagree can still parent successfully. Kids are much more perceptive and flexible than you think. Every day they relate to a whole bunch of adults who hold differing ideas on how kids should behave and who have varying discipline policies. Kids in any elementary school can give you the "lowdown" on each of the teachers and can tell you how they can and can't behave with each one. Certainly kids can do the same at home where they need only relate to two adults. Some of the ways to avoid danger when parents use different parenting techniques are:

• Don't let the kids play one parent off against the other. When one parent says no to a request, kids often ask the other parent, hoping for a yes. Don't say it! Or when a child is disciplined by one parent, he may run to the other for sympathy. Don't give it! Resist becoming involved in any situation that is between your spouse and your child. Allow them to solve the problems that arise between them by themselves.

• Do not criticize your spouse's parenting methods. Each parent needs to be able to interact with the child as he or she sees fit.

• Don't use your spouse's unwillingness to adopt your methods as an excuse not to make a strong effort on your own to solve problems with the children.

• Be careful not to displace onto the child any feelings of anger and resentment you may experience when your spouse refuses to do things your way.

• If you and your spouse frequently find yourselves in major disagreement and confrontations over parenting techniques, see if there is a lack of agreement in other areas of your life together. Sometimes difficulties in raising kids mask fundamental difficulties in the husband/wife relationship. As long as the focus remains on the children, the parents avoid an honest confrontation with the underlying marital difficulties. Try solving the marital problems before attempting to reach agreement on parenting issues. Seeking help from a professional counselor may be wise.

Resist Unhelpful Outside Interference

Nothing will make it harder for you to persist in your efforts to discipline your child in new ways than unwanted interference from outside parties. Friends, neighbors, and relatives seem to love to criticize and to predict disaster when someone tries a different approach. It is especially difficult to listen to remarks from older people whose own kids were raised successfully in the authoritarian tradition. "Make them behave," they will tell you, "Show them who is boss." Listen to enough of their comments and you will feel like an absolute failure as a parent, and your resolve to learn new techniques of parenting will weaken.

You rarely can convince someone to change an opinion by arguing about whose ideas are correct. This pursuit often ends with everyone angry at each other. You don't need anyone else's approval, whether a neighbor or a mother-in-law, to discipline your children as you see fit.

Discourage unwanted outside interference with a short comment such as "This is the way I have chosen to discipline my children. Thanks for your advice, but I plan to do things my way." Then change the topic of conversation.

Plan Helpful Outside Support

Ever notice how much easier it is to exercise regularly when you are a part of a group than when you do it alone? Being part of a group also makes it easier to learn new parenting skills.

Meeting regularly and talking with other parents who are confronted with similar situations and who are attempting to make the same types of changes can be very encouraging. You can congratulate each other on the successes and work through the problems together. You can sharpen your perceptions of children's misbehaviors by talking over the various situations presented in this book. You can explore the various recommended techniques until you feel comfortable that you understand them and can apply them correctly. You can discuss the ways of applying the different techniques to your individual situation.

Such support groups are particularly important to single parents, who do not have another adult in the home to turn to for encouragement and for advice. A group comprised of all single moms or all single dads could provide not only support for dealing with the kids, but also help in dealing with other situations and problems unique to single parents. All you need to start such a group are a few interested parents, a commitment of one night a week for a couple of months, a book for each participant, a cozy living room, and a willingness to share.

3

· ·

Mealtime Madness

Mealtime! It can be the most pleasant time of day for a family. Breakfast can be a time when the family shares a few minutes together before each person goes off to his own world of work or school. Dinner or supper can be a time when all are assembled together again, ready to share their experiences of the day.

Unfortunately, for many families, mealtimes turn into unhappy times filled with squabbles and chaos that leave everybody upset. Kids fight with each other, fuss over their food, whine, and complain. Parents yell, threaten, and occasionally send misbehaving youngsters away from the table crying.

Let's find out how parents can cope with mealtime misbehaviors and enjoy peaceful meals.

Greetings   The first time family members greet each other in the morning or after school or work is an important moment in the maintaining of close relationships. A warm greeting. accompanied by a touch on the shoulder or a hug or a kiss says "You are important and I care about you." Even though these first moments are often busy ones for parents, spending that little bit of extra time together is easily repaid by the amount of good family feelings that result.

Reasonable Expectations

It's helpful for parents to have a clear idea of what mealtime behaviors can reasonably be expected from their child.

Children in the five–twelve-year-old range can be expected to come to the table on time, washed and ready to eat. They can sit at the table for up to thirty minutes without jumping up and running around. One bathroom trip can be permitted, yet even that shouldn't be necessary very often. The kids can be civil toward siblings and can participate in the family conversation. Like adults, kids have varying moods, so some days they'll seem more lively and eager to participate than other days. By school age they should have mastered the art of using a fork, knife, and spoon effectively, although occasional spills and messes will occur. They will have food dislikes and preferences just as adults do, and they may be hesitant to try new foods. Yet they needn't express dislikes in continuous complaints, demands for special foods, or loud refusals to eat anything that's served. At the end of thirty minutes they can be expected to have finished eating and to clear their dishes from the table.

Should friends ring the doorbell or call on the telephone, the kids can be taught to reply, "We're eating now. Please come back or call back in thirty minutes."

On Cleaning the Plate

Q. Do you believe in insisting that children eat everything that is on their plates at the table?

A. No. I believe the less fuss you make about what your children eat, the fewer problems you will have at mealtime.

The role of parents is to make nutritious food available to their children for meals and snacks. Notice the difference between making the food available and insisting that the kids eat all the food served in the amounts the parent feels are appropriate. It is not the role of the parent to force a child to eat everything that is served at every meal. In fact, such attempts to force a child to eat usually result in balky, picky eaters who hassle their parents at every meal.

Notice also that making nutritious food available does not mean catering to each person's likes and dislikes. It is not necessary for parents to be short-order cooks. Don't feel obligated to provide alternatives to suit all tastes. Do rotate your menus so that each person's favorites appear eventually and that particular dislikes don't appear continuously.

Eliminate snacks if you feel your kids don't eat well at mealtime. There's nothing like an empty stomach to convince a child to eat what's served.

If your children consistently leave food on their plates, have you considered that perhaps you are giving them too much food? It's common for parents to overestimate the amount of food a young child needs. Many of us equate giving food with loving and nurturing, so we urge our children to eat more than is necessary. Check with your children's pediatrician. If he or she does not find the kids underweight, then either cut back the amount of food you give them or don't insist that they clean their plates.

Better yet, why not put the food on the table in large bowls and let the kids help themselves? Provide small serving utensils and small plates if the kids tend to take too much food.

Children like to have control over this small area of their lives. Then they can regulate how much they eat according to their own body needs. Some days they may be very hungry, other days not hungry at all. It's important for children to recognize and respect the signals that their body gives them. A lot of weight problems adults face are caused by ignoring the natural body signals of hunger and satiation.

Endless Eater Needs Limits

Q. My daughter, age seven, takes a full hour to eat dinner every night. She pokes at her food, makes a couple of trips to the bathroom, fools with her sisters. By the time she is done, I'm a nervous wreck from nagging and yelling at her, and the rest of my evening is ruined. Should I ignore her because some children are just naturally slow, or is there a way to make her eat faster?

A. I don't think there is a trait called "naturally slow" that is passed along through genetic inheritance. Children often learn to eat slowly and to dawdle, however, as a way to gain special attention from parents or to engage parents in a power struggle.

Make a decision regarding how long dinner will remain on the table in your house. Thirty minutes should be enough time for any child to eat. Before the next meal, sit down with your children and explain that mealtimes are taking too long. Explain that from now on the table will be cleared at the end of thirty minutes, and no more food will be served until the next morning. In a calm, friendly voice explain that it is their decision how quickly or slowly to eat, and that you no longer will remind or nag them to finish. If you place a portable kitchen timer set for thirty minutes on the table, it will help the kids to judge the time.

At dinner that night, clear the table without a word at the end of thirty minutes. If there is still food on your daughter's plate, give no postmortem lecture on why she should have eaten faster, and make no prediction about how hungry she'll be later. Remember, silence is golden when a parent is taking appropriate action.

If your daughter comes to you later complaining of hunger, be friendly, acknowledge her feelings, and let her know you're looking forward to seeing her at breakfast. Do not engage in a long discussion about eating. Do not feel sorry for her; she will not starve by going to bed hungry. You need not feel like a terrible mother because your child is hungry; it was her choice to eat very slowly.

As soon as your daughter is allowed to experience the consequences of slow eating, she will learn to eat her dinner in the allotted time.

Make Peace with Picky Eater

Q. How can I get my child to stop being such a picky eater? I've studied a bit about nutrition and know the foods my child is supposed to be eating. But I'm losing the battle in getting these foods down his throat!

A. You will lose, as long as mealtime is approached as a battle. Whether we like it or not, a child is in control of what goes into his mouth and what is swallowed! Yet there are ways to entice a child into wholesome eating habits.

One way is to give a child some choice of what is to be served. The scope of the choice depends upon the child's age. A two-year-old can be given a choice between two or three different kinds of cereal in the morning. A nine-year-old can sit with a parent and help plan the weekly menus. Planning menus is the best time, by the way, for teaching a child about nutrition. It's the time for discussions about what foods must be eaten and what proportions are necessary to maintain a healthy body. If you attempt to teach the kids about nutrition at the table, particularly when they are refusing to eat something, the kids will see this as your attempt to coerce them to eat an unwanted food. They will resist this coercion mightily. Vary your menus as much as possible, and serve different items from each food group on different days. Thus, if your children avoid certain fruits, for example, a fruit that they do like will be served soon at another meal.

Another way to change a picky eater's habits is for the parents to serve only healthful, nutritious foods for both meals and snacks, to let the child eat what he wishes, and not to be concerned if the child refuses to eat a certain food. A child who misses part or even an entire meal occasionally will not starve. A given meal might be unbalanced. Your child might even go through a period during which he avoids a certain kind of food entirely. But when only nutritious food is served, a properly balanced diet will most likely result if considered over a few days or weeks. If you are particularly worried about a poor diet, keep a journal of the foods your child eats in a week. This will help you judge objectively just how balanced the diet really is, and will allow you to stay out of the battle line over food.

Don't insist that your kids try a bit of everything, especially with a new food. The less pressure they feel, the more willing they will be to try new foods.

Don't use dessert as a bribe to get your kids to eat other foods. By doing this, you teach your kids that some foods are rewards and others are to be eaten only for the sake of getting something better. They learn to see the main course as a prelude to dessert rather than a good meal for its own sake. If the dessert is nutritious like the rest of the meal, it can and should be available to everyone, regardless of what they have already eaten.

Set the example by eating all foods served yourself. A child who constantly hears Mom or Dad refusing various foods will assume that he has the same prerogative. Parents achieve the most cooperation from their children when there is no double standard in the home, when the same rules and standards apply to all.

Family Fights Fat Together

Q. My ten-year-old daughter is overweight. Is she too young for me to put her on a diet? Unfortunately, her eating habits are very fattening. She loves sweets of all kinds, as well as potato chips, pretzels, and all the fattening stuff that kids like today. I'm afraid it will be quite a battle if I tell her she can't eat these things, especially when she sees the rest of us eat them. But I know kids are beginning to tease her because she is fat. What's the best way to get a child to lose weight?

A. You are right to be concerned about your daughter's weight problem. Overweight children tend to become overweight adults. Parents need to do something about a child's weight problem as soon as it is noticed, in the hopes of heading off this lifelong tendency towards obesity.

First, as with any physical disorder, check with your pediatrician. Make sure there is no medical problem of which obesity is only the symptom.

Most weight problems are caused by a combination of poor eating habits and insufficient activity. More calories are consumed than are burned up. That's a simple fact that most people with weight problems prefer to ignore.

A diet is a temporary solution for losing weight, and not usually a very effective one. The dieter makes an attempt, for a given period of time, to consume fewer calories and thereby lose excess weight. Once the weight is lost, and the diet is discontinued, the original pattern of overeating and insufficient exercise returns and the weight is put back on. Book stores are filled with the latest bestselling diet books. If any of them worked permanently, we wouldn't need so many new diet books each year. Since most adults can't successfully and permanently lose weight through dieting, it's not very realistic to think that a child can. Putting a child on a diet also puts too much negative attention on his problem. This can become a weapon in the child's hands. Whenever he wants to upset his parents, all he has to do is reach for the potato chips.

The solution to a child's weight problem is to change the eating and activity habits of the entire family. Easy to do? Of course not. But the rewards are many. Everyone will feel healthier when meals and snacks consist of only healthful foods. Switch to fruit, vegetables, unbuttered popcorn and unsweetened juices for snacks. Substitute fresh fruit for rich desserts. Drink skim milk, cook more lean meats, chicken, and seafood, and serve lots of raw and cooked vegetables. Watch the sugar content of canned and processed foods, especially breakfast cereals. Don't keep any junk food in the house.

You'll also have to increase the vigorous activities your family engages in. If your family already enjoys an activity, such as walking, swimming, or skating, increase the time you spend doing it. Gradually add one or two new activities that all members of the family agree they would like to do. Think of the benefits not only to everyone's physical fitness, but to the closeness of your family as you share more fun activities.

In today's sedentary world, with the wealth of calorie-laden food all around us, it's not easy for anyone, child or adult, to stay trim and fit. By focusing on family fitness, rather than on one child's weight problem, everyone in the family will enjoy better health and the overweight child will receive the support needed to lose weight.

Squabbling over Squash

Q. We have a lot of vegetables in our garden right now, but at least one of my kids complains and refuses to eat whichever vegetable I've decided to cook. Is it wrong to insist that the kids eat these vegetables? We've had some unpleasant fights at the dinner table over this issue.

A. It's not wrong to expect the kids to eat the vegetables. The way you are going about it, however, by insisting, sets up a power struggle that apparently makes many meals unpleasant.

Consider it a given fact that vegetables from the garden will be served. Within that given, there are some legitimate choices the kids can help make.

One choice is how the vegetables are prepared. Sometimes the vegetable kids won't eat as a plain steamed dish will be gobbled up in a casserole. Cookbooks are filled with tasty vegetable recipes. Some kids prefer vegetables raw, either plain or in salads.

Another choice is how the vegetable is served. Special dishes make a food seem more desirable. These dishes need not be expensive. Garage sales are great places to pick up extra dishes.

Still another choice is the frequency with which a vegetable is served. Make a week's schedule with the kids, so that it becomes automatic which vegetable is to be served and it won't be mother's fault that "we're having carrots again." That way everyone knows what's being served, and it will also be obvious when one's favorite vegetable is on the menu.

Spillers Sponge the Spills

Q. My kids are very clumsy at the table. They spill food as they take it from the serving bowls. They frequently knock over juice or milk glasses. I'm tired of cleaning up their messes!

A. Good. I'm glad you're tired of cleaning up their messes. You can stop doing that today. The people who should be cleaning up the messes are the people who make them.

Kids can clean up spills from serving bowls with sponges or paper towels. You can avoid some of their messes by paying careful attention to the type of serving utensils you use. Ladles and plastic measuring cups with long handles used in place of spoons make it easier to scoop food without spilling.

> **Teach Your Children** Never simply assume children know how to perform a task you set. Take the time to teach them.

Keep a small plastic bucket and a couple of sponges handy in the kitchen. Anyone who spills juice or milk can get the bucket and clean up the mess. Teach your kids how to do this some afternoon when you're not too busy. Then when messes do occur at mealtime, just remind them to get the "spill bucket" if they don't hop up and get it by themselves. The best way to teach kids not to spill things is to let them experience the consequences of cleaning up. You'll ruin the lesson, however, if you make angry comments about their clumsiness.

Table Talk Is for Everybody

Q. My wife and I would like to have pleasant conversations at dinner. I have a lot to tell her each night about my day at work, and I like to hear about her day. My problem is that our kids constantly interrupt us. How can I get them to stop interrupting and to concentrate on eating instead?

A. Don't use the dinner hour to share news and ideas with your spouse that won't be of interest to the kids. Share these either before or after dinner, when you can have some well-deserved time alone. Some parents relax with coffee after dinner, after the kids have gone out to play, are busy with homework, or are watching TV. It's nice for parents to have each other's undivided attention while talking.

At dinner time, the kids want to be part of the conversation. If you don't include them, they will most likely misbehave to get your attention. They'll interrupt, or complain about the food, or spill something accidentally-on-purpose.

Occasionally you just might want to let your kids eat early

so you and your wife can share a meal by yourselves and enjoy uninterrupted conversation together.

Discourage Junk Food Junkies

Q. Is it possible to break the junk-food habit that my kids have developed? I know that the soft drinks and candy and potato chips they like are nutritionally bad for them, but they pester me until I give in and let them eat what they want. How can I keep them from reaching for the junk?

A. Simple—don't buy and keep junk food in the house. If it's not in the cupboards or the refrigerator, they can't reach for it. But neither can you! And that's the hard part.

If you really want to wean your kids from junk, you must be willing to follow a good diet yourself. Supply the model but don't preach. Your kids will learn much more from watching you than from listening to you.

Explain to the kids that junk food is too costly in terms of both money and health for you to continue to buy it. Together make a list of some healthful snacks that could be kept on hand for hungry kids, and keep plenty of items from this list available.

It won't be possible for you to control the amount of junk they eat when they are not at home. In fact, the more you try to do this, the more resistance you will probably get from the kids. But the model and example you set at home will be powerful lessons for them.

The Snack SNAFU

Q. After-school snacks are a real problem around our house. The minute my kids come in the door after school, they announce they are starving. But everyone wants something different, so by the time they go out to play the kitchen is a wreck.

In addition, my oldest daughter keeps snacking all afternoon and then doesn't want her supper. Yet if I take away the snacks, everyone complains. They also complain because I try to limit the sweets and won't buy some of the junk-food snacks they ask for. What's a parent to do?

A. A little organization ahead of time will solve your problem. First, sit down with your kids and make a list of all the foods that would be suitable for snacks. You do not have to provide junk foods; there is no proven correlation between eating sweets and having a happy childhood. The snack-food list might include dried fruits and nuts, fresh fruit slices, milk and cheese products, peanut butter and whole wheat bread, whole grain cookies, popcorn, and unsweetened juices.

Next, make a calendar that shows the next three or four weeks. Decide together on one or two items that will be available for snacks each day. If that decision is hard for your family to agree upon, write each snack on a piece of paper and choose the papers at random. List each day's snack on the calendar and post it prominently in the kitchen. This will eliminate every child demanding something different.

The next decision to make is how long the snacks will be available. A thirty-minute time period should be ample time. After the allotted time the snack food is put away. This will eliminate kids snacking until dinner time and then refusing to eat supper.

By deciding in advance what snacks will be served, and by providing only healthful snacks that help fulfill the child's daily nutritional needs, and by limiting the time during which snacks are available, you will be able to eliminate the problems you are having when the kids come home from school.

Avoid Trouble at the Holiday Table

Q. Thanksgiving is upon us, and my husband and I are nervous when we anticipate the trip to my parents' home for the traditional turkey dinner. Sometimes we are very embarrassed by our children's inappropriate manners and behavior. Is there any way I can assure myself that they will behave this year?

A. Appropriate behavior at a holiday dinner is a matter of training and advance planning. Have a practice session before you leave home. Set the table with empty plates and bowls. Let the kids role-play the grandparents while Mom and Dad role-play the kids. Model the language you would like them to use in accepting or rejecting food. Switch roles and let the kids practice using the language they have just heard.

Here are some other tips to make the meal go smoothly:

• Avoid unpleasant power struggles over what the kids eat by letting the children decide for themselves which foods they will eat. A holiday dinner is not the time to stress the values of vegetables and a balanced diet. Let the kids also decide how much they will eat.

• Place the kids between adults at the table, rather than at one end by themselves. Also, seat the kids next to other relatives than their own parents wherever possible. Include the children in the dinner conversation, even the young ones. Leave the exclusively adult topics for later over coffee, after the kids have gone off to play.

Uninterrupted Dinner   Dinner hour is often the only time the family has to be together. Don't let this valuable time be constantly interrupted by the telephone or the doorbell. If neighborhood children are in the habit of ringing your doorbell looking for playmates, put up a sign that says "Dinner being served. Please come back after ____ o'clock." The phone can be answered with "We're at dinner now. Please call back at ____ o'clock." Or take the phone off the hook at dinner time. Your family will value these times together if outside interruptions are minimized.

Raw Vegetables Some youngsters complain of being hungry before dinner is served and beg for snacks. For anyone who just can't wait, accommodate this annoying behavior by having a bowl of raw veggies ready. Include any combination of carrot and celery sticks, cherry tomatoes, cauliflower and broccoli heads, green pepper rings, cucumber slices, and so forth. The snack itself is so light and healthful that it won't matter if the kids eat their fill.

Clearing the Table Everybody eats, so everybody should help clear the table. Any child old enough to sit on a regular chair at the table with the family is old enough to carry his or her own dishes from the table, scrape them, and stack them appropriately. Adults are old enough too. If you clear your own dishes after eating, the kids will follow your example.

Kids Cooking Teach each child in the family to prepare certain "specialties" for the family to enjoy. It cuts down on the parents' work and it increases the child's self-esteem. Give each child his own small metal box in which to file recipes. Children feel good as they watch their files expand.

Points to Remember

Recognize the power struggles that occur when a parent says *eat this*, and the child, by his stalling or picky behavior, says *you can't make me*.

The more attention a parent gives in coaxing or forcing a child to eat something, the more payoff the child gets by refusing.

Serve only healthful, nutritious foods, for both the main course and dessert. Then if your kids choose not to eat a particular food, they can have a nutritious meal by eating everything else.

Involve the kids in planning, cooking, and serving meals.

Involve the entire family in pleasant mealtime conversations. Don't use this time to nag, criticize, or solve difficult problems.

4

••

Bedtime Bedlam

It's 7:30 P.M.. The kids are playing quietly or watching TV or doing homework. You think to yourself that if only the kids would troop off to bed tonight with no hassles, you'd finally be able to sit down and relax after a long day of work. But past experience tells you that things are not going to go so smoothly.

The kids are happy doing what they are doing. They ignore you when you request that they get ready for bed until you begin screaming or threatening them. When they finally start to get ready, they take forever to get undressed, washed, and into pajamas. It's hard to be patient now; your energies have faded away along with your hopes of some quiet evening time for yourself. At long last the kids are in bed, ready for their bedtime story. You realize that if you can hold on for just a few more minutes this will all end. Finally the story is over; everyone has been kissed and tucked in; the lights are out. As if on cue, the requests start. "Can I have a glass of water?" "Can I go to the bathroom?" "I'm scared. Can I sleep in your bed?" What happened to the so-called joys of parenthood? you wonder, as you slump down in the sofa and pray they'll get tired of yelling and will soon fall asleep.

Reasonable Expectations

You can set a specific time for each child in your family to be in bed and expect that child actually to be in bed at that time. There is no specific time that will be appropriate for all six-year-olds, seven-year-olds, or others. Children's needs vary; you will have to set the time based on your own observations of how tired your child gets during the evening, how easily he falls asleep, how early he wakes up in the morning. The older children in your family will probably have later bedtimes than the younger ones. When your child is ready for it, usually sometime between the ages of twelve and fourteen, you will want to let him choose his own time to go to sleep, although you may still have a specified time for him to be in his room for the evening so you can have some well-deserved private time uninterrupted by children.

While parents generally are happy when bedtime approaches, children usually are not. Most likely they are enjoying whatever it is they are doing and have no desire to stop and go to bed. Younger children don't yet understand the

---

Changing Activities When you know a change of activity is going to occur, give your child a fifteen-minute notice before the new activity must begin. This allows the child a chance to finish whatever he is doing before complying with your request. You'll find your child is much more cooperative when not asked to do something "this instant."

Appreciation Exchange Set up a time in the evening, perhaps just before bed, when your family can exchange appreciations with each other for all of the good things that happened in
the day. You'll be teaching your kids two important skills by
doing this. They will learn, first, to notice what other people do
and, second, to express their feelings about what they have
noticed. How nice it would be if parents could actually hear
their children expressing thanks for the many things parents do
that seem to go undetected. Many times the kids do notice, but
just never get around to saying anything. By your setting aside
a special time to exchange appreciations, everyone can end the
day feeling warm and loved.

---

connection between how late they stay up and how they will
feel the next day. Nor do they understand that parents need
peace and quiet and some uninterrupted time. So you can
expect them to voice complaints and disappointment when
you announce that bedtime has arrived. However, you can
also expect that, despite their disappointment, they will get into
bed at the appropriate time.

Thirty minutes is plenty of time for a child to undress,
wash and/or bathe, and dress for bed. Children under seven
may need some involvement from you in bathing and getting
ready. Children older than seven can generally be expected to
bathe and get into pajamas by themselves.

All children like special attention from their parents just
before they go to sleep. Some like stories, some like songs,
some just like to talk. Expect to spend a few minutes each night
with each child before you kiss and tuck him in. Once they
have each had that last kiss though, you should be able to turn
your attention to other things. You do not have to return to
their rooms with extra drinks or help them to the bathroom or
shoo away imaginary monsters that just happen to appear five
minutes after you've settled down with a good book. You can

safely ignore all of these manipulations they use to get you to spend a little more time with them.

Occasionally, *very* occasionally, a child will have a bad dream or nightmare and will require parental comforting. If these bad dreams become too frequent, however, it is rea sonable to expect the child to learn to handle his own fears without your nightly presence.

Beat the Bedtime Battles

Q. Bedtime is a problem in my house. I can get my kids into bed by 8:30 with few hassles, but then the trouble begins. One son wants a drink of water. Another complains he's not tired and can't get to sleep. Often it's after 10 before all the children actually fall asleep. By then it's too late for me to enjoy my evening. How can I make my kids fall asleep soon after they get into bed?

A. You can't.

Remember the old saying: "You can lead a horse to water but you can't make him drink." You can make the kids get into bed but you can't force them to fall asleep. In fact, the more you pressure yourself or someone else to fall asleep, the more difficult it is to actually get to sleep. Ask any insomniac. Consider also the variations in sleeping patterns among adults. Some fall asleep easily, some toss and turn for hours. Some can get by with only five or six hours of sleep and others need nine or ten hours. The same differences in sleeping patterns exist among children.

Now that you've considered the facts of sleeping, let's look at your needs as a parent.

By 8:30 at night, you feel the need to be finished coping with kids for the day. Most likely you're anticipating an evening of adult companionship and/or some enjoyable activity, or just time to yourself. Let's see how we can balance your needs as a parent with your children's needs to fall asleep when they're ready.

Continue putting the children to bed at 8:30 with the understanding that once they are in bed that is where they stay. Put a thermos filled with water on a table next to the bed of any kid who is always thirsty. That way there is no need to call Mom or Dad for permission to get up for a drink. Give each child a high intensity night lamp next to the bed or mounted on the headboard; allow quiet reading until the kid feels ready for sleep. If you have more than one child in a room, give each child a nightshade to wear over his eyes if he is bothered by the light.

Music also may help the children to fall asleep. Sometimes it's hard to find quieting music on the radio; you might want to use records or a tape. If you attach a pillow speaker to the radio or recorder, your son will have to keep his head on the pillow to hear the music. Most likely, sleep will soon follow.

Will the kids stay up all night? Not often, if you allow them to experience the natural consequence of being tired the next morning without any extra sympathy, service, or lectures from you. Breakfast is served at the same time as usual. If the kids are too tired to get up and dressed quickly, they simply miss breakfast. They will soon learn the relationship between the time they decide to go to sleep at night and how they feel the following morning.

Appropriate Attention   Be sure to give your child the encouragement of lots of attention when the child shows positive behavior. So many moms and dads notice the kids only when they misbehave, thereby reinforcing the negative behavior. When the kids are being good, how about a hug or a word of appreciation for them. The more attention you give kids while they are behaving appropriately, the less misbehavior there will be.

Serve Snacks Before Bedtime

Q. My children always seem to get hungry after they have been put to bed for the night. We eat supper early, usually at 5 P.M. so perhaps it is reasonable for them to be hungry again around 8 P.M. But when they ask for food after they have been put to bed, they interrupt my evening which I would like to have for myself. Am I being selfish? Do growing youngsters really need an extra snack at bedtime?

A. Let's separate the issues of adequate amounts of food for the kids and their annoying bedtime behavior.

Your children might indeed need an extra snack in the evening if dinner is so early. Why not serve this snack at your convenience instead of theirs? Have it ready for them after they are in their pajamas and before they brush their teeth.

Give them the choice of eating a snack at this time or waiting until breakfast in the morning. State clearly that a snack after they are in bed is not a choice and that all requests at that time will be ignored.

What your children have been doing is keeping you busy with them during your evening time, which you deserve to have for yourself. No, the desire to be away from your kids for a while is not selfish. It is a legitimate need that all parents experience.

When you fulfill this need, you will have more love and energy to share with your kids the next day. When you deny your own needs, you will feel drained and will most likely resent your kids the next day.

Difficult Dreams

Q. My nine-year-old son woke up the other night crying about a dream he was having. In his dream he was fighting with his little brother and at one point in the dream picked up a baseball bat and hit his brother over the head. I ended up almost as upset as he was because I don't want my children even to think about hurting each other. How can I best handle a situation like this if it should happen again?

A. Children often have thoughts and dreams that cause them and their parents great anxiety. Often these are about hurting others, dying, monsters, or scary happenings. Many children feel so guilty about having thoughts or dreams about hurting others that they don't dare tell their parents or anyone else about them.

The first thing for you and your son to realize is that there is a difference between thoughts and deeds. The fact that we think or dream about something doesn't mean we are actually going to do it. Often we may have little conscious control over our thought processes, but we do have conscious control over much of our behavior. Thinking is not doing. Dreaming is not doing. Tell him that his thoughts and dreams are okay but that actually hurting others will not be allowed.

Assure your son that he is not a bad person for having these thoughts and dreams, that it is normal for all of us to have thoughts and dreams about things that we will never actually do. Tell him that this happens to lots of people and he is not different or bad.

Encourage him to talk about his upsetting thoughts and dreams with you. Listen attentively and accept what he says. Don't criticize or judge. You can even share some unwanted thoughts and dreams of your own. Looked at in the light of reality the unwanted thoughts and dreams will not seem so scary.

Minimizing Monster Fears

Q. Our five-year-old daughter is giving us a hard time at night. She doesn't want to go to sleep because she says there is a scary monster that comes into her room at night. We have given her a night-light. We have left the door open. We have even nailed the window shut! Yet sometimes she keeps calling to us for as long as two hours after we have put her to bed. How do you deal with such childhood fears?

A. When a child repeatedly expresses an irrational fear, be unimpressed. In your daughter's case her fears conveniently allow her to stay up an extra two hours. She also keeps both parents busy with her, comforting her and trying to solve her problem.

The first time a particular fear is expressed, listen to your child and let her express all of her feelings. Then express your faith in her ability to handle the situation by a statement such as "I'm sure you can figure out what to do about the monster. Let me know what you decide."

If the same fear is expressed again and again, respond with a short, humorous remark such as "I bet no other kid has a monster for a friend," and immediately turn your attention elsewhere. Avoid continuous involvement so she learns that others cannot be manipulated by fearful behaviors.

So when bedtime arrives, put your daughter to bed in the usual manner. Kiss her goodnight, express your faith in her ability to handle "the monster" and let her know you won't return to comfort her during the night.

Child Prefers Parents' Bed

Q. I have a child who says she is afraid to sleep alone in her room, so for the past couple of years I have been letting her fall asleep in my bed. It seemed to work okay in the beginning. Before we went to sleep either my husband or I would carry her to her own bed and she'd continue to sleep through the night. Now that she is five she has begun to wake up when we attempt to move her and she cries and screams to stay with us. Our evenings are a real hassle now and by the time we go to bed we end up cross with each other. How can we get her to go to sleep in her own bed?

A. I'd like to use your letter as an example for other parents for it demonstrates how the proverbial ounce of prevention will save much grief later. Parents often let little ones who fuss at bedtime into the parents' bed because the kids quiet down more easily there. The parents assume the kids will outgrow the behavior eventually.

While some kids do outgrow it peacefully, for others sleeping in the parents' bed often becomes a habit, something they think they are entitled to do. Attempts to break this habit can spark a real battle of wills. The best way to combat this is to let them know you have confidence in their ability to sleep alone and not to let them in your bed in the first place. Let them express and talk about their fears but don't be manipulated into taking them into bed with you night after night.

In your case the behavior is already well established and it will take real determination and courage on your part to break it. I urge you to break it, for this behavior is not helpful to your child and is especially harmful to your relationship with your husband. You have a right to enjoy the late evening hours by yourselves.

Ask your child what she needs to help her sleep alone in her bed. Don't try to talk her out of her fears; they are real to her. Let her express them but let her know you believe she can learn to cope with them. Once you have listened to and supported her and have made plans together for her to sleep alone, be prepared to follow through. Re-read the section entitled "Expect Occasional Unhappiness" on page 9. The first few days she may be upset, cry, even throw a tantrum, or give you the "pitiful me" routine. Realize that she will experience a wonderful lesson in growing up and a great gain in self-confidence when she develops mastery over her fears.

Performing for Company

Q. My six-year-old son causes trouble when we have company for the evening. When we put him to bed he never stays put. He keeps popping up and coming into the living room with one request after another. He fools around and acts silly. The company usually laughs at his antics and gives him a lot of attention, which doesn't help any. I'm embarrassed by his behavior and would like to know if you can suggest a way to get children to stay in their beds when company is present.

A. Children often refuse to go to bed when guests are present because they miss their normal bedtime routine. Mom and Dad are not available for the usual story or bedtime talk. Sometimes children will remain in their beds if their parents go through the entire bedtime routine earlier in the evening. Explain to your son that when guests are present you are not able to read or talk at bedtime but will be glad to do these things ahead of time, perhaps just after dinner. Later, when the guests are present, he is to play quietly in his room. Set an alarm to go off when it is time for him to stop playing and get into bed.

An extra incentive to staying in bed is a pillow speaker attached to a cassette tape recorder. For nights when company comes, prerecord a special story that you are sure will keep your son's head firmly on the pillow so he can hear it. After the story, record a special good-night message just for him.

Occasionally let your son also have company for the same evening your company is present. His company is a hired babysitter, one who lives close by and can walk home after your child is asleep.

Ask your company for their cooperation in helping to eliminate your son's disturbing behavior. Explain the problem, and ask them to ignore your son, to pay no attention to his silly antics. It won't take your son long to realize it's no fun being a clown when nobody notices.

Bedtime Closeness As kids get older they outgrow the desire to have a bedtime story read to them or to be cuddled and tucked in before they go to sleep. When this happens, don't give up the closeness that comes when you spend the last few minutes of the day together. Sit on the side of your child's bed and use these minutes as a time to talk and share. This can be a comfortable time to share private thoughts that don't come up at more hectic times during the day. And no child (or grown-up either) is too old for a hug, kiss, and an "I love you" before his eyes close.

Art Books In place of the usual story at bedtime, consider occasionally looking at art books with your child. The public library has many oversize books with excellent reproductions of the world's finest paintings. Take the time to share your reactions to the paintings.

Closed Doors Some parents don't like to close the bedroom door on a young child. They want to be able to hear easily if anything happens. They also like to be able to look in without disturbing the child. You can have a door that is both open and closed by sawing two feet off the top of the door. While a young child is shielded by the lower part of the door from distractions outside the room, a parent can easily look over the top. And a child's noises will travel easily through the top space. You might even want to saw six inches off the bottom so a favorite family pet can get in and out.

Announcing Bedtime No one likes to be told what to do, especially if it means one has to stop an activity one is happily engaged in. When parents tell children they must get ready for bed, the kids are often unwilling to listen. One way to sidestep the power struggle that frequently arises between a parent and child at this time of day is to let a kitchen timer or an alarm clock announce bedtime to a child old enough to understand time. Give your child about fifteen minutes advance warning so he can wind down his activity before getting ready for bed. Set the alarm for fifteen minutes and make it clear that when it rings he is expected to get ready for bed. Leave the clock where your child can see it so he can check as often as he likes to see how much time is left. There just isn't the same satisfaction in arguing with an alarm clock as there is in arguing with a parent!

Prebedtime Activities To help your child fall asleep easily at bedtime, plan prebedtime activities that are relaxed and calming. This is not the time for horsing around or getting all keyed up playing competitive games. It is a time for reading together, singing quiet songs, talking softly, or even snuggling up to watch a favorite TV show together. If you set up a daily bedtime ritual that includes one or more of these activities, you will find that sleep will come much more easily. This ritual is usually eagerly anticipated by the child and thus helps overcome any resistance to bedtime.

Pillow Flashlights Some children who express fear of the dark are comforted by having a small flashlight under their pillow when they go to sleep at night. Then they can use it to check out any ominous shadows that are scaring them without calling for Mom or Dad or hopping out of bed to turn on the overhead light. When you let them handle their fear of the dark by themselves, you are demonstrating your belief in their ability to be self-reliant. And self-reliance is one of the building blocks of self-esteem.

Switching Parents In two-parent families, it's nice if the parents can take turns supervising the child's bedtime preparations and participating in the bedtime rituals such as stories and lullabyes. Then the child is assured of sharing some special time alone with each parent each week. This deepens and strengthens both parent/child relationships.

Points to Remember

Stick to the schedule. Bedtime, once decided upon by your family, is a constant. Don't renegotiate each night based on the whims of anyone in the family, parent or child. Evenings when the family is out together are the exception. Agree beforehand on your return home and stick to it.

Enjoy the closeness that comes from spending the last few minutes of each child's day together.

Consistency counts. Once the last goodnight has been said, refuse to be sucked into returning to the kid's bedside except in case of an emergency.

The best place for kids to sleep is their own beds, not the parents' bed.

Be unimpressed by repeated nighttime fears. The purpose of most nighttime fears is to manipulate the parents into giving extra attention at an inappropriate time.

5

. . . .

The Three Rs: Rules, Routines, and Responsibilities

"Jimmy, wake up! Time to get ready for school. Susie, hurry up and finish getting dressed; your breakfast is getting cold."

Getting the kids up in the morning and ready for school on time is a real headache for many moms and dads.

Nighttime is often just as difficult. "Jimmy, put away your toys and go take your bath. And don't leave your dirty clothes on the floor. Susie, did you remember to brush your teeth? Hurry up and get into bed or you'll be tired in the morning."

By the time the kids are finally settled for the night, after the last call for a drink of water and good-night kiss, many moms and dads are too tired to enjoy the remainder of the evening.

And then there are all the frustrating times during the day when parents cajole, complain, and threaten in an attempt to get their kids to help around the house.

"Susie, come in here right now and set the table. This is the fifth time I've called you. Jimmy, it is your turn to do the dishes. Turn off the TV until you get them done. And don't forget to take out the garbage, especially the bag from last night that's still sitting in the kitchen."

Is there anything more annoying than having to remind a child over and over again to do a simple chore?

"Mama, all you ever do is nag at me!"

Sure you nag at the kids. If you didn't nag, would anyone except you ever do anything around the house?

In many homes today, both parents work. Time is scarce; there are barely enough hours in the day to clean the house, do the laundry, put meals on the table, and still have a bit of time left to spend with the kids. For a one-parent family, this time crunch is even more severe. How much easier it would be for everyone if the kids took responsibility for a share of the household tasks, willingly and without endless reminders.

Reasonable Expectations

Kids will allow you to do for them what they really should do themselves. They will let you be their personal morning wakeup service and evening bed- and bath-time assistant. They will gladly accept your cooking, cleaning, and washing clothes for them. No kid seems to object to enjoying all of the privileges and benefits of being a family member while avoiding all of the work and responsibilities involved.

Children who are old enough to go to school can begin assuming more and more personal responsibilities and household chores. To get kids to carry out their responsibilities you will need to establish rules and routines appropriate to their ages and capabilities and set up specific consequences for failure to conform to the agreed-upon rules and routines.

As you read all of the questions and answers that follow, it may seem at first glance that too many schedules, routines, and structures are being suggested. It does take a lot of planning, organizing, and following through to make the suggestions work. But the rewards for your perseverence are real. Your rewards are more time and more energy for other aspects of family life, for relaxing and playing together, for hobbies and favorite activities. Not having schedules and structures means dealing with each and every problem as it occurs, as a new and separate problem that must be figured out and dealt with on the spot. Not having schedules and routines means flying by the seat of the pants, without well-thought-out plans laid ahead of time.

Allow some flexibility in following through on routines and consequences, for there are legitimate emergencies and extenuating circumstances that do arise and require occasional shifts in plans. But be extremely vigilant that occasional flexibility doesn't lead into a pattern of repeated skipped responsibilities and avoided consequences. As you begin to apply the suggestions in this chapter, it is better to be too firm rather than too flexible. You can ease up later on when all is going smoothly.

You cannot expect kids to be able to do every task perfectly the first time around. Though parents frequently say, "It's easier to do it myself," it is really only easier for the moment. The short-term goal of peace at any price is

---

"Here, Let Me Do That"   Parents, throw this sentence out of your vocabulary! How discouraging it is to a child who is fumbling with a task to have a parent take it away and do it quicker and better. The lesson the child learns is that he surely has poor skills and little value. Self-confidence flies out the window. Instead, use an encouraging phrase that will give your child the patience to stick with the task until success is achieved. Say, "Wow, I like the way you keep at it until you've got it," or "It often seems hard when you're learning how to do something. You're doing a good job of learning."

achieved, but the long-term goal of responsible, helpful children is subverted. Expect, initially, to take time to teach your children to do chores. If added up in minutes, the amount of time saved by future help will far exceed the amount of time spent teaching the kids to do these chores. Don't expect your kids to always be cheerful and happy about helping. Do expect your kids to help regardless of their negative feelings.

Keep the benefits of assigned household responsibilities in mind when you run into the inevitable rough spots and have to set unpleasant consequences to teach kids to carry out their responsibilities.

Continue the Consequences

Q. I have made several changes lately in the way I deal with family problems based on the idea of limited choices and consequences. My twelve-year-old son is not happy with these changes. He likes making his own choices but reacts very negatively when experiencing any type of negative consequence. He claims all this new stuff I'm doing is just a different way of bossing him around. What's wrong?

A. It seems you are experiencing a perfectly normal reaction to a change in parenting style. As stated in Chapter 1, most children are not too pleased when parents begin to change their parenting style because they have been successfully manipulating us to get their own way for a long time.

By the age of twelve a child is feeling a strong desire to think for himself and to become independent, so a parent's use of limited choices in guiding behavior is perfectly appropriate.

The best way a parent can guide a child to become skilled in making appropriate choices is through the use of consequences, which children at this stage in growing up would prefer to avoid. As the old saying goes, they want to have their cake and eat it too. But such is not the way of the world. For every choice they make there is a consequence, sometimes a desired consequence and sometimes one they prefer to avoid. What your son is saying is that he wants choices but no unpleasant consequences no matter what he chooses. The consequences are there, whether or not he wants to avoid them. It's a lesson he must begin to learn now.

His remark that you are bossing him around is an attempt to manipulate you by making you feel guilty, so that you will intervene and take away the unpleasant consequences of his choices. Don't do it!

Household Chores Are for Everyone to Share

Q. How can I get my kids to help with the household chores?

A. Let's first define household chores and then look at some guidelines for encouraging kids to help with these chores in a responsible manner. It can be done.

A distinction needs to be made between household chores and tasks related to personal care. Household chores are all of the tasks that must be done to keep the family functioning smoothly. Tasks related to personal care include personal hygiene, cleaning bedrooms, picking up toys, cleaning up accidental messes, and so on. These are personal responsibilities and should not be included in a list of household chores.

The household is the child's first adventure in group living. Here the child learns that he not only receives benefits from group living but that he is also expected to contribute to the well-being of the group. He discovers that every family member is affected by how well each person in the family performs his chores.

The entire family should be involved in the planning of chores so each member will feel a personal responsibility to see them carried out. Hold a family meeting to plan when and how chores will be done and who will do them. Begin by listing

Commenting on Contributions One way to encourage your children is to notice their contributions to family life and to make positive comments about specific helpful behaviors. In making such comments, state both the behavior that pleased you and the effect the behavior had on you. For example, suppose your child surprised you by folding the family wash. An appropriate comment might be "Gee, I'm really pleased you folded all the wash. Now I have more time to relax with the family tonight."

This type of comment gives the child specific information on what behaviors are pleasing and helpful. When a child hears such a remark, he translates the parent's pleasure internally into feelings of self-confidence that heighten his self-esteem.

on a large sheet of paper all of the chores that must be done in order for the family to function. Include everything, even the chores that only parents can do, such as paying rent, shopping, and so forth. This list will prevent future complaints of unfairness by letting your kids see some of the invisible things that parents have to do. It will also educate the kids in all of the factors that go into running a household.

Next, check off the items that only parents can do. Then let the kids help decide who will do each of the remaining chores. Be flexible and allow them to choose some of the more creative chores, even if it means Mom or Dad has garbage detail for a while. Write down the decisions concerning when and how each chore will be performed as well as who will do it. Kids and parents both choose until all of the listed chores are accounted for. All decisions are binding until the next scheduled family meeting. At that time new decisions can be made, chores can be rotated and consequences established for anyone who is shirking his duties.

When parents have problems getting their kids to do chores, it is often because the kids resent being told what to do. Amazingly enough, when planning is shared with the kids

"Me Do It My Way" The very young toddler attempting a new task frequently refuses to follow a parent's suggestions. The toddler wants to figure it out for himself, to try different solutions, perhaps to discover a solution different from the one the parent has in mind. In other words, the toddler wants to do it his own way. Parents need to encourage a child's desire to experiment and find his own way to do things, whether the child is two or twenty. Any goal can be reached by many paths and it is a sign of intelligence, creativity, and spirit when the child devises his own path. Encourage these traits in your child by giving him such affirmations as "It's okay to do things differently sometimes," and, "It's okay to figure things out for yourself."

and they are given choices and responsibility, they show a wonderful ability to be reliable and responsible.

R-o-u-t-i-n-e Spells Security and Relief

Q. How important is it to be consistent and do things at the same time each day? I like variety in my own life and don't like to stick to routines and schedules. Even if I want to be consistent, with all the different activities going on in our family, it's hard to plan ahead. Will it make any difference if we just take each day as it comes without a tight structure?

A. Dr. Rudolf Dreikurs, in his book *Children: The Challenge* says: "Routine is to a child what walls are to a house; it gives boundaries and dimensions to his life. Routine gives a feeling of security."

The purpose of consistency and structure in household routines is to establish a calm, serene atmosphere where each person knows what is expected of him. The smaller the children and the larger the family, the more important the routines become. For a child with any type of handicapping condition, consistent routines are absolutely essential.

Routines and structure allow parents to teach their children to be cooperative and responsible through the use of consequences rather than punishment. For example, if a child fails to come home on time for supper, he misses the meal. The consequences of hunger experienced for a short time will teach the child the value of being responsible for getting home on time. Or, if a scheduled clean-up is not completed, the child may not move on to the next activity which might be watching a favorite TV show. Thus the consequence of not completing a chore is missing a favorite activity.

When the family establishes these routines together, everyone in the family will feel that he is an important part of the household. Each person will know exactly what is expected of him and will be aware of the consequences of shirking these responsibilities.

Teach Responsibility Through Consequences

Q. What are reasonable, effective consequences for kids who agree to do a certain chore and then either forget about it, do it poorly, or simply refuse to do it at all?

A. Before you use any consequences, discuss them at a family meeting. Let the children offer their suggestions for appropriate consequences, and have each child choose which consequence he prefers. Remember that the child only gets to choose *which* consequences will occur, not *whether* a consequence occurs.

It might be that at the family meeting your children devise consequences just as effective as those I suggest. In that case, use them. Here is a list of four possible consequences for not doing chores:

1. A related task from which the child benefits is left undone. For example, if the table is not set, dinner is not served. If the kitchen is not cleaned or the garbage is not put out, no one cooks in the messy kitchen. Say nothing, just busy yourself in another activity.
2. The next activity doesn't occur. By scheduling chores before such pleasurable events as dinner, evening TV, or recreational activities, you give kids a good incentive to perform the chores responsibly.
3. Someone else does the job and whoever missed it must pay back the time, with interest, at the other person's convenience. A variation of this consequence is to have the parent do the child's chore in place of something that the parent does exclusively for the child's benefit, such as chauffeuring the child to a friend's house or to a recreational activity.
4. The child is awakened about an hour after he has fallen asleep to do the chore. I have to confess, this one sounds a little cruel to me, yet one of my own children chose this a few years back and I found out just how effective it is!

Exchanging Jobs Is Okay

Q. My daughter hates to clean up her room. A few days ago when I was nagging her to clean up the mess, she asked me if I would clean her room if she took care of another household job instead. She offered to clean the kitchen cupboards, which I hate to do, while I cleaned her room. This seemed fair enough to me so I said okay. The problem is that her father thinks I am letting her get away with murder by cleaning up her room. Do you think I made a mistake?

A. No. As long as your daughter did an equivalent amount of work, and you would rather clean her room than clean the cupboards, I think you found a good way to solve the problem of her messy room.

Allowing children a choice, whether in clean-up tasks or other household responsibilities, builds goodwill and cooperation in the family. Be aware, though, that kids cannot choose to do nothing. They must participate in household clean-up activities.

All of us have some household jobs we prefer over others. I, for example, would much rather clean up from a meal than cook. This preference coincides with those of other family members who would rather cook than clean up.

If two members of your family can agree on what seems to them a fair exchange of jobs, encourage them to switch. An exchange of jobs does not affect other chores, and each person is expected to assume responsibility for completing all other assigned tasks.

Don't Assume Kids' Responsibilities

Q. What can I do when my daughter doesn't set the table on time for supper after she has agreed ahead of time to accept that responsibility? I've got enough to do getting the dinner ready and I feel resentful when I have to nag and remind my daughter each and every day.

A. No wonder you feel resentful, for the actual responsibility of setting the table is falling on your shoulders instead of hers. Since you have made an agreement, it is now solely her responsibility to carry out the chore. Stop reminding her. As long as you remind her, she needn't remember for herself. Instead, try either of the following techniques:

1. Do not serve dinner at the usual time. Turn off the stove, leave the kitchen, busy yourself elsewhere. If anyone asks what you are doing and why supper is

not being served, simply announce matter of factly that you can't serve dinner on an unset table. Say no more. Your message will come across loudly and clearly.

2. Someone else sets the table for her. She must pay back the time involved, with interest, at another time.

3. Change the time for setting the table so that she can do it right after school, when you can spend some "special time" with her. Probably she feels left out of the supper process because you are busy preparing the food.

Notes, Lists, and Schedules

Q. Last Saturday I had to be away from home for the entire day visiting my sister who was ill. Before I left I wrote a note to my kids, ages fourteen, eleven, and nine, listing jobs that needed to be done around the house. When I returned, much to my surprise, all of the jobs were done. Normally I have to nag and threaten the kids all day to do their chores. Why on earth do they seem more responsible when I'm away than when I'm home?

A. How nice for you to discover how cooperative and responsible your kids can be when they choose to! I hope you noticed and commented on all the completed chores. Kids often help out willingly in a pinch like this because they sense they are needed, and out of the sensitivity that all children possess, your kids responded appropriately.

There is another lesson to be learned from your experience, however. That lesson is that you can win cooperation by avoiding direct verbal orders and confrontations. Let a note, schedule, or list tell the kids what to do instead.

There seems to be a part of each of our personalities that is like a rebellious child. When we are directly told to do something, this rebellious child part of us often instinctively responds, "No, I won't." In some children the rebellious child is very meek and not seen often, but in other kids it is seen all too frequently.

You can avoid tangling with the rebellious child part of your children when you learn to lead and guide them indirectly rather than attempt to coerce your kids with direct orders. Your note did exactly that.

Writing notes, posting schedules, making lists work because they sidestep the power struggles that so often occur between parents and children. A child will talk back and argue with a parent who reminds or orders him to do something. But what fun is there in arguing with a list? Looking at notes or lists is an objective, nonemotional way of being reminded what to do. This gives the child a feeling of control over his own life.

Alarm Clock Tells Kids to Get Up

Q. How can I get my child up in the morning without coaxing, nagging, and yelling?

A. The good old alarm clock works wonders for getting children up in the morning. Take your child shopping and allow him to choose his own personal alarm clock. There are many interesting, fun styles to choose from. Even a kindergarten child can respond to the buzz of a clock that he has set himself. Parents and children together can decide what time the clock needs to be set so the child has enough time to dress without extra help from the parent. Allow the child to experiment with earlier and later times so he can experience consequences resulting from the decision. Some children like to set their clocks earlier than parents think necessary because they like to move slowly in the morning. Others prefer to set the clock later, and rush. These are legitimate decisions for the child to make. Allowing a child the right to make personally significant decisions at an early age prepares the child for making important decisions later.

Beat Bath-Time Battles

Q. What suggestions do you have for avoiding hassles at bath time? We're down to three or four baths a week instead of daily baths simply because the struggle involved to get our kids to bathe was too much to get through every day.

A. To sidestep the struggle over whether or not your kids will bathe you can provide limited choices of when and how they will bathe. Remember, not to take a bath at all is *not* one of the choices.

Bathing three or four times a week is probably enough in winter unless children are involved in a sweaty gym activity daily at school. Choices over when to bathe are made by sitting down with the kids once a week and letting them decide which days they will bathe during that week. The kids then write their choices on the family calendar.

Choices over how to bathe can include the following:

1. Bath or shower.
2. What kinds of soap (keep plenty of different kinds available).
3. Which washcloth and towel to use (beach towels with attractive designs often will appeal to the child).
4. How long the bath or shower will be (a kitchen timer can be set and placed in the bathroom).
5. What kind of after-bath products to use (powder, skin lotion, deodorant, and so forth).
6. What time of day for bathing (morning, evening, after school, before dinner, and so forth).

By providing limited choices of when and how to bathe, you are allowing your child a chance to make decisions and to feel in control of small areas of his life. The more small areas a child feels in control of, the less need the child will feel to challenge the parents over the control of large areas.

Use Grandma's Rule

Q. All of my friends have the same problem with their kids—messy rooms! Do you know any families who have solved this problem?

A. When my own children all lived at home I found it useful to establish a specific clean-up time each week. Otherwise I found myself becoming irritated every time I noticed a messy room. Just knowing that a scheduled clean-up time was coming made the rest of the week seem more bearable.

Our clean-ups were scheduled for Friday afternoons. Dinner on Fridays was always pizza, for all family members (parents too) whose rooms were clean. For anyone who chose not to clean, and once in a while that did happen, dinner was a peanut butter sandwich.

Other families I know set the clean-up time for Saturday morning before the TV cartoons. The same principle applies: the logical consequence of not cleaning the room is to miss the favored activity that immediately follows.

You might ask your kids to help decide upon the specific time the weekly cleaning will occur. Establish the consequence for failure to clean at the stated time.

Setting up such routines and consequences is an application of Grandma's Rule: *First we work, then we play.*

Who Decides When Clean Is Clean?

Q. I have been following your suggestion that kids clean their rooms before a weekend activity they all enjoy. Together we decided to do room cleaning on Saturday mornings before the

---

Thought for the Week   Never do for a child what a child can do for himself.

cartoons come on TV. We run into trouble when they announce they are finished and call me to inspect the rooms, for the rooms are never really clean and neat enough by my standards. The kids say they should decide for themselves how clean and neat their own rooms need to be. I say there have to be general standards for everyone in the family. Who is right?

A. You'll have a better chance of solving this problem if you stop thinking in terms of who is right and who is wrong. Think instead of possible solutions that everyone can agree to live with. To win the kids' cooperation, keep the following pointers in mind:

1. Make a very specific list of just what is expected to be done. List exactly what needs to be put away, dusted, and vacuumed. Also list how often a specific job needs to be done if some jobs, such as dusting bookshelves, need not be done each week. Involve the entire family in making these lists. Moms and dads who are super neatniks may have to bend a little.

   For a child too young to read a list, make use of pictures instead of words. Let the kids help make these lists of pictures.
2. Bind everyone, including parents, to the rules and standards that the family agrees upon. It is a great example for the kids when they see their parents performing the same chores at the same time.
3. Rotate the job of "inspector." Let the kids take turns, when they are old enough, inspecting the rooms of other family members, including parents. You might take some snapshots of the room in acceptable condition and use these pictures as a reference for how the room should look.

Puppy Care

Q. For our son's birthday a few months ago we surprised him with a puppy. For the past two years he had been pleading with us to let him have a dog, promising he would take care of the dog all by himself so we wouldn't have any extra work. We finally gave in, thinking that because he had waited so long he would really follow through with his promises to take care of his pet. Well he does care for the pet, but only after endless nagging on our part. How can we get him to live up to his original promises?

A. A pet benefits the whole family. All can enjoy sharing love with a pet, receiving unconditional love and acceptance in return. This is especially important for kids who often make a pet their confidante and constant companion. When he cares for a pet a child gets to explore the role of caretaker and protector, a switch from his usual dependent position. This experience can increase his ability to relate to and care for other people.

Despite children's fervent promises to take care of the pet all by themselves they rarely follow through. Though their intentions are sincere, young children often do not have the ability to carry through with such an ambitious program. The job of the parents is to help set and monitor the routines for the animal's care, while most of the work is done by the kids.

Routines for feeding the pet, walking it, and cleaning up the pet's messes should be connected to other daily events in the child's life. Walking and feeding the pet can most easily be tied to the child's own mealtimes. Establish a rule that the pet is walked and fed before the child is served his breakfast or dinner. When you establish such a routine you won't need to nag constantly to make sure that the animal is fed. An empty plate in front of the child should be reminder enough.

Cleaning up the pet's messes can be tied to some daily event that the child looks forward to, such as an evening playtime or TV show. Establish the rule that the pet's messes must be cleaned up before the child can play or turn on the TV. For unexpected messes that the pet makes around the house, you need to designate someone to be the pooper-scooper, someone who stops what he is doing and cleans the mess as soon as it occurs. Rotate being pooper-scooper among all family members.

When you set up routines such as these for animal care you turn over to the kids the major responsibility for their pet within a structure that their age allows them to handle.

Neat Beds To simplify bedmaking, consider using a fitted bottom sheet and a sleeping bag instead of two sheets, blankets, and spread. Even a preschooler can tug a sleeping bag neatly into place. If you coordinate a solid color sheet and pillowcase with a print or plaid sleeping bag, the bed will look attractive. Today's sleeping bags can go into the washing machine the same as other linens. For hot nights, it's easy to make a light-weight sleeping bag, particularly if you have a sewing machine. Buy four yards of cotton flannel and fold in half with the selvages (woven edges) forming the long sides. Sew up the sides, hem the tops and you have a summer bag.

An Alarm Clock Any school-age child can benefit from his own alarm clock. An alarm clock frees the parent from the responsibility of waking the child each morning. It also allows an older child to determine for himself what time to get up.

Sudsy Dishwater To avoid a mess of dishes left in the kitchen by family members who like evening snacks, leave a pan of sudsy dishwater sitting in the kitchen sink for the evening. This pan will make it easy for snackers to clean their dishes instead of just dumping them in the kitchen sink.

Chores on Cards If your child is expected to do chores after school, reminding him about them the minute he arrives home is not the most effective method. Instead, jot the chores on note cards and have these cards waiting for the kids on the table along with an afternoon snack. You might even go one step further and have the kids help decide once a week which chores need to be done when. They can then write out their own chore cards to be left on the table each day.

A Calendar or Appointment Book All sorts of attractive calendars are available. Choose one with a theme that will interest your child. Display the calendar in a prominent place, perhaps on the refrigerator or on the child's bedroom door. Write on the calendar all of the activities that are regularly scheduled on the appropriate day, such as bedroom clean-up, household chores, bed linen changing, clothes sorting and putting away. Let the child do as much of the writing and scheduling as possible. Older kids might appreciate a pocket-size appointment book in addition to or instead of a wall calendar. Teen-agers can keep track of not only family responsibilities but also music lessons, sports events, doctor and dentist appointments, and their own social engagements.

It's amazing how much more readily a child will respond to a calendar telling him or her what to do than to parental reminding. This is true because arguments and power struggles with a calendar are pointless. The calendar also represents to the child another important milestone in taking charge of his own life, thereby enhancing the child's self-image.

Junior Janitors Young kids, especially preschoolers, love to play with water, sponges, soap bubbles, and so forth. They also love to imitate parents. Put the two together and let your youngster help with house cleaning. Buy an inexpensive plastic caddy for junior and equip the caddy with a sponge, dish rag, powdered cleanser, and inexpensive dish detergent. Give the child a demonstration of how each item is used on a sink, then let junior wash all the sinks in the house. You will be surprised at how much young kids enjoy activities that seem like chores to an adult.

Thank You Notes One way to get kids to remember to do specific jobs around the house—without nagging—is to post

Belonging For a child to be happy and have a good self-image, he or she must feel a strong sense of belonging within the family. This sense of belonging develops when a child feels he or she has a worthwhile contribution to make to the family. It's not easy to make this contribution in our gadget-filled lives, where children are no longer needed to carry out essential duties for the survival of the household. The successful parent finds creative ways to help each child make a unique contribution to the welfare of all by using his or her special talents, interests, and abilities.

appropriate thank you notes in strategic places. How about "Thank you for not leaving dirty dishes" posted over the kitchen sink or "Thank you for hanging up the towels" in the bathroom. Use these notes in whatever areas are trouble spots in your home. To make the notes attractive and conspicuous you might try making them out of circles of colored construction paper with a smiling-face design. Better still, get the kids to help make them on a rainy day. Change the notes regularly—they lose their appeal if left for months on end.

Avoid Direct Commands You can avoid confrontations and power struggles with your kids by changing direct commands into impersonal comments when it is time for them to do something. You'll have much more success if you say, "The clock says it's time for a bath," rather than "Go take your bath now." You can announce rules in this same impersonal fashion. Say "In this house everyone washes his hands before dinner," rather than "Go up to the bathroom and wash those dirty hands." Most of us, adults included, balk when we are told directly what to do. You sidestep this tendency to rebel when you avoid direct commands.

Points to Remember

Maintain consistent daily routines to provide security for your children and to teach them responsibility.

The more involved kids are in establishing routines and assigning chores, the more they'll follow these routines and actually do the chores.

When a child fails to do an agreed-upon chore, avoid the impulse to do it yourself.

An unpleasant consequence is the best response to an undone chore.

The more a child learns to do for himself, the greater his self-confidence and self-esteem. Make it your motto never to do for your child what he can do for himself.

6

Concerning Clothes

Morning is a hectic time for everyone. Kids have to wash, dress, eat, and get off to school; parents have to prepare themselves for work. How much easier it would be if parents did not have to help their children pick out and put on clothes, if kids could dress on their own without fussing about it!

Nighttime is often just as busy. Supper must be cooked, the house straightened, laundry washed. How much easier the latter chore would be if all the dirty clothes were in the hamper where they belonged instead of scattered over floors, under beds, behind dressers!

Caring for clothes is a personal responsibility, something each person must do for himself. When parents turn this responsibility over to their children, they will have more time to take care of their own needs and responsibilities.

Reasonable Expectations

The child in kindergarten or first grade may need a parent's help choosing appropriate school clothes. By second grade, he is old enough to choose the clothes he is going to wear each day by himself. You can expect any school-age child to dress without dawdling and fooling around and to be ready for breakfast on time.

It is reasonable to expect dirty laundry to be put in the hamper, not strewn around the kids' rooms. A child five or older can empty hampers in the laundry room and sort the clothes by color. Put a stool near the washer and the same child will be able to put the sorted clothes in the machine. Most six-year-olds, with some supervision, can measure and add the soap and turn the appropriate dials. Wait until your child is ten or eleven before you let him add bleach because of the danger of this harsh chemical splashing on his skin. By age ten a child can sort fast- and slow-drying clothes and transfer wet clothes from the washer to the dryer.

All school-age kids can be expected to fold and put away their own clothes. Perhaps each item won't be folded as perfectly as Mom or Dad could fold it, but if perfection isn't demanded, the child's ability to do chores such as fold clothes will improve.

As the kids get a little older, they can be expected to mend their own clothes. Replacing buttons, sewing a simple ripped seam, ironing on patches—all can be mastered by age twelve.

When you go shopping, even a five-year-old will want to pick out his own clothes. Given a limited selection to choose from, your child will enjoy making the final decision for himself. As the child gets older, he'll be able to choose from a larger selection. By age twelve your child will probably want to choose without your interference, though you will want to set dollar limits on his purchases.

You Wear It, You Wash It

Q. I have recently taken a full-time job for the first time. With three children at home, ages five, ten, and eleven, I'm experiencing how hard it is to find the time to work and still do all the things I used to do around the house. One job I have a hard time getting around to is the laundry. One of my co-workers says she lets her kids do their own wash. Do you think kids the ages of mine could be expected to wash their own clothes?

A. If you have your own washer and dryer, there is no reason why not. Even a five-year-old can measure soap powder, push buttons, and turn dials. Teaching your kids to do their own laundry is beneficial for all concerned. You will save time and energy. Your kids will develop greater self-esteem and self-confidence. They'll be pleased that you are sure enough of their capabilities to trust them to use the washer and dryer correctly. They'll feel grown-up taking on adult responsibilities. They will be learning the skills they need for independent living when they leave home. I recommend that all parents transfer this responsibility to their school-age children.

How you actually turn over the task of washing clothes to them is very important. Don't tell them they will *have to* do laundry as an extra chore because you no longer have time. Explain instead that you have realized that they are old enough, mature enough, and capable enough to wash their clothes by themselves.

Take the time to teach them proper use of the machines the first few times they wash. Teach the younger children to measure accurately. If you use such additives as powdered bleach (safer than liquid bleach) or fabric softener, show your kids when in the washing cycle to add them and how to handle dangerous chemicals safely. Teach them how to remove stains before they wash. Teach them how to separate their clothes into different washes by colors and fabric, or take the easy route and use a cold water soap which allows all colors to be washed together.

Dawdling over Dressing

Q. I've got a six-year-old daughter who dawdles over dressing. She'd still be in her room at lunch time trying to pick out her clothes or sitting with one sock on if I didn't constantly nag her and partially dress her myself. At what age should you expect kids to dress themselves in a reasonable amount of time?

A. Certainly by the time she goes to elementary school a child should be able to pick out her own clothes and get dressed with no help from Mom or Dad.

To shorten the time it takes her to get dressed in the morning, have her choose the next day's outfit the night before. If your youngster has trouble making this decision, give her limited choices. Take out perhaps three blouses and say, "You can wear any one of these blouses. You decide." Sometimes the process of choice is a hard one for children to learn and by limiting the choices for a while you build up their skill and confidence in making choices.

If she is still too slow getting dressed, don't remind her or nag her or do it yourself. Just set up a rule that breakfast is served during a certain time each day, only to kids who are dressed and ready for school. If she dawdles, the consequence is that she misses breakfast. No "I told you so." Just tell her, "I'm sorry you missed breakfast today. Perhaps tomorrow you'll decide to dress a bit more quickly." She won't starve. She will learn to dress more quickly.

Long Sleeves or Short?

Q. What can you do with a nine-year-old boy who never seems to dress appropriately? On warm days he puts on heavy shirts with long sleeves. When it's cold he picks out his thinnest clothes and would go outside like this if I didn't remind him to take a sweater or a jacket. Isn't he old enough to know better?

A. Of course he is! However, by dressing inappropriately it seems he has found a good way to bug you and keep you busy with him.

By age nine, choosing proper clothing is a task that belongs to the child. He is old enough to make the connection between the weather and his clothing. When he picks poorly he will experience natural consequences that will teach him to choose more wisely. If he's hot, next time he'll learn to dress more lightly. And there is nothing like feeling chilly to convince a person to grab a sweater, or sitting all day in wet sneakers to teach a child to wear rubbers.

These natural consequences won't teach the child anything if the parent interferes. Don't nag him, remind him, or tell him what to wear. No "I told you so" if he chooses incorrectly; instead, let him know that you have confidence in his ability to choose wisely, then stay out of it. It may take a while before he is convinced that you really won't interfere, that it's really his decision. When he does understand this, however, he will learn for himself to choose more appropriately. Mistaken choices today will lead to more appropriate choices tomorrow if consequences are allowed to occur.

Realize, though, that body reactions to heat and cold differ among different people and he might make choices that you would not make. Trust him to figure out his own body needs.

When a Jean Is Not a Jean Is Not a Jean

Q. My twelve-and-a-half-year-old son will only wear certain types of jeans that cost from $18 to $20. He will not consider the less expensive brands. He does his own washing weekly but he would skip it if I didn't insist. He is willing to wear the same clothes days and weeks on end. I think that he ought to have four or five pairs of jeans so that none are worn more than twice without washing and so they will last the school year. He wants the kind he wants and doesn't care about washing them or making them last. I am sick of the issue. I really don't know what the most reasonable thing is for me to do. I do know I won't spend $100 on jeans for him. What is a reasonable solution?

A. When we hit a problem such as this one it often seems as if there are only two possible solutions—either buy the jeans so the child is satisfied, or don't buy them so the parent is satisfied. In either case, one person "wins" and the other "loses." Any such win/lose situation ends up with one person unhappy, and the parent/child relationship suffers as a result.

The secret to solving this type of problem is to realize that you can find other solutions if you take a closer look at the problem. It is just possible that one of these additional solutions will be acceptable to all involved so that each person will end up feeling okay and like a winner.

The way to find all the possible solutions or alternatives to solving a problem is to brainstorm. Brainstorming is a technique that all ages can participate in; it is the key to creative thinking. To brainstorm ideas, have everyone involved sit down with a large sheet of paper and a magic marker. Write down every possible solution each person can think of. These possibilities don't have to seem sensible or feasible to all. Do not allow comments or judgments about the possible solutions suggested. Do allow "piggybacking," a suggestion of an idea only slightly different from one that someone else has suggested. It's often this kind of small adjustment that makes one solution acceptable while a similar one is not. The last step in brainstorming is to choose from the many ideas written down the one solution that is most acceptable to the people involved. If there is no such acceptable idea, it simply means you must brainstorm some more or find other people to help you brainstorm. The more possibilities you come up with, the better your chance of finding an acceptable solution.

Here are three possible solutions to your problem with the jeans.

1. Let your son have the jeans he wants but spend only what you would have spent on a less expensive brand. Let him pay the difference out of his allowance or savings. If he has neither, let him earn the money by doing extra work around the house.
2. Give him a budget for all his clothing needs for the next few months and let him help make some decisions about how to spend the total amount. He may be willing to spend less on other clothes, perhaps even buy some clothing in a second-hand store or scrounge for hand-me-downs from relatives or friends in order to have enough money left to buy the jeans he wants.
3. Buy only two or three pairs of jeans instead of four or five with the agreement that he will wash them more frequently and will wear patches if needed for the jeans to last the school year.

Do sit down with him and brainstorm other possibilities before you choose the solution.

Let's Lose Less

Q. My children constantly lose small articles of clothing at school. They have lost hats, mittens, sweatshirts, and gym shorts. Given today's high prices, I'm tired of replacing lost items. Is there any other solution?

A. Yes. Parents should not reward carelessness by constantly replacing lost personal items. Since it is the child who has been careless, it must be the child who replaces the items.

Depending upon the age of the child, the replacement costs can be handled in a number of ways. Older children who baby-sit or hold outside jobs can be expected to use their own funds. The same is true for a child whose allowance is sufficient to cover replacement costs.

Children who do not have enough personal money to replace the items can be expected to perform extra household duties to earn part or all the replacement costs. These chores should not be ones that are part of their regular routine. For example, the child could wax a floor, clean a cupboard, or wash the car. For the younger child it is sufficient for the child to earn only part, not all, of the replacement costs.

Once your children realize that they have full responsibility for their personal articles, that Mom and Dad aren't going to replace the things they lose, they will have a much greater incentive to keep track of their belongings.

Pajama Problems

Q. Have you ever heard of a kid going to bed in tomorrow's clean clothes instead of pajamas? My son insists on doing this because it "saves time" the next morning. I suppose it does, but sleeping in clothes seems odd to me and completely freaks my mother out when she sees it. Do you think I should insist that he wear pajamas instead?

A. Nightclothes are a matter of custom and preference, and I'm afraid I really can't give you a good reason for having him switch to pajamas, provided his clothes are wrinkle-proof and thus don't show the night's wear.

This situation is an example of a child making a decision that is very different from the one a parent would make. Our usual reaction in this situation is to insist that the child do things the "proper way", that is, "our way." Yet often there are no harmful consequences from the child's action, either to himself or to his parents, or to his grandmother. Ignore her interference and reaction.

When you allow him to control this small area of his life you begin to build his confidence in his own ability to make decisions for himself, a vital skill in becoming an independent adult.

Laundry Relief   Tired of folding and putting away laundry for the whole family? Buy each person a plastic laundry basket to be kept near the washer and dryer. When clothes are finished put each person's things in his or her own basket. Clothes that wrinkle easily can be draped over the side of the basket. That evening have each person take his basket to his room where each can fold and put away his own clothes.

Clothes Hampers   Does your child often throw dirty clothes on the floor instead of using the family hamper? If so, you might find that a special personal hamper kept next to his bed solves the problem. Take him shopping with you and let him pick out the hamper. Or make a hamper out of a large carton that he paints and decorates himself.

Paper-Doll Training   If you have a youngster starting school next fall, begin teaching the child to choose appropriate clothes. Play together with paper dolls, explaining as you dress the dolls which colors and designs go well together. Have "make-believe" days with different weather conditions so the child can practice choosing raincoats, sweaters, and mittens. It's acceptable for little boys as well as girls to play with real and paper dolls. Have an assortment of paper dolls on hand so your child has some choice over which doll to dress.

Name Tags   Help prevent the loss of mittens, scarves, and hats by making sure each item has a name tag in it. Name tags are easy to make. All you need is seam binding and a laundry marker. Let your child write his own labels. Elementary-school children can even attach the labels themselves with a simple sewing stitch.

Boot Ease Plastic food storage bags over shoes make damp boots easy to slip on and off. Also have your child keep a clothespin in his coat pocket for clipping his boots together in the school closet.

Mittens Attach one end of a long piece of yarn to each mitten of a pair and slip one mitten through your child's coat sleeves. This prevents the mittens from accidentally falling out of pockets and being lost.

Choosing Clothes Children deserve some choice over what they wear. We all have personal preferences and want to follow our preferences as far as we can in our lives. When you let kids make choices in all areas in which they are capable they will fight you less over decisions you must make for them.

Keep the clothes choices within reasonable limits by presenting three or four possible items that differ in color or style and allowing the child to make the final decision.

Fighting Fads All kids seem to have certain kinds of clothes they like. These clothes are usually very different from the clothes you wore when you were a kid. Don't fight the fads; let your kids dress in the style their friends follow even though it's not what you want them to wear. How to dress is a decision

Verbalizing Instructions When you ask a young child to perform a task, have the child verbalize back to you just what he or she is going to do. That way you'll know whether or not the child has heard correctly and has a clear idea of your expectation. Give a toddler only one simple instruction at a time. As the child experiences success with one instruction, try two at a time. By increasing slowly, you minimize the chances of your child being frustrated by a task he or she is not able to handle. Giving simple verbal tasks to a preschool child helps develop the reading-readiness skill called auditory memory.

that rightly belongs to the kids; it is the way they express their personality and their independence. The more you attempt to fight the fads, the more they'll insist on dressing that way.

"Mom, Fix It" Part of growing up is learning to fix and mend your own clothes. All children need to learn this skill. Teach your young children to sew on buttons and to apply simple iron-on patches. As they get older they can learn to use a sewing machine to repair ripped seams. Remember, never do for a child what he can do for himself.

Points to Remember

Set routines with built-in consequences to teach kids to dress in a reasonable amount of time.

As your kids get older, increase their freedom of choice. When they decide what clothes to wear and buy, don't impose your own preferences for colors and style on them. Let them express themselves through their clothes.

Use the language of privilege instead of the language of drudgery when you teach them to wash and mend. Don't *make* them do anything—*allow* them to do it. They are getting older, more capable, so the privilege of participating in these activities is now theirs. After all, it can be exciting to learn how to use machines that are usually operated by adults only.

Stay involved with your kids as they wash and mend their clothes. It is much more fun to do these things in the company of Mom or Dad.

Give your kids lots of encouragement. Praise their abilities to choose and take care of their clothes and make positive statements about their growing capabilities to take care of their needs.

7

· ·

Childhood Can't Always Be Happy

It is late at night and your children are all sound asleep. You can't resist stealing a peek—what angelic faces they have! Is this the same boy who came home so angry and frustrated three hours ago because his team lost the Little League game? Is this the same girl that was crying and upset earlier because you said she couldn't visit friends after dinner on a school night, the same girl who screamed that you make her life miserable, that you're unfair, that she'll lose her friends just because you said no?

When you see them sleeping you wonder how they can be anything but pleasant and loving, how they could ever show an unpleasant feeling. One day everything seems to go so smoothly with them; they are happy and cheerful. The next day somehow things go wrong and the tears flow. To make matters still worse, you never know when these changes in mood and behavior will take place.

Reasonable Expectations

Every child comes into the world able to experience a full range of emotions. As parents, we are delighted when our children experience joy, happiness, anticipation, patience, confidence. We are not so delighted when they experience sadness, jealousy, fear, pain, frustration, anger, boredom. To be fully human, however, is to experience all of these feelings. Both children and adults can be expected to show a full range of emotions.

Adults generally react predictably in given situations. Expect feelings and behavior in kids to be much less predictable, much more erratic, especially as the child nears the teen years.

There are many natural circumstances in life that may frustrate a child or make him miserable. It's unreasonable for parents to think that their child can escape such situations, for many are beyond parental control. Just think how much of a child's life is spent away from home in school, among teachers and other children. The older a child gets, the more influence his peers have. It becomes less and less possible for his parents to shelter him from life's unpleasant situations.

You can expect a child to grow in his ability to cope with unpleasant situations and to handle negative emotions. Unlike

---

Encourage by Affirming Encourage your child to become self-accepting and self-confident by giving him affirmations. Affirmations are powerful statements that say that it is okay to think, feel, or behave in a certain way. These may be verbal statements, in which case a parent uses words to express approval of what the child is doing. Affirmations may also be nonverbal, in which case the parent indicates approval by a certain look, a hug, a smile, a touch, or special attention. By giving kids affirmations, we give them the information they need to make decisions about themselves upon which their personality is built.

physical growth, however, this emotional growth is not a steady progression. There will be periods when your child appears to cope very well with unpleasant events, followed by periods when everything seems to fall apart. In the preteen years these changes occur so rapidly that a situation adequately handled today can bring tears and anger tomorrow.

Cashing in on Illness

Q. My ten-year-old daughter has been home from school for three days with the flu. While she steadily improves, I am definitely getting worse. Her constant demands for attention, drinks, and entertainment are running me ragged. The first few requests I answer pleasantly, but by the time she has asked for the twentieth glass of water I am ready to scream. Is it necessary for me to respond to all her calls for help?

A. No, it is not necessary for you to respond to each and every one of her demands. In fact, by giving her so much extra attention and by allowing her to boss you around, you are teaching her that being sick has some very pleasant side benefits. Many people learn to use illness to get love and attention that could best be obtained in other ways. Give your sick children no more attention than is necessary to insure healthy recuperation.

Don't do for your daughter what she can do for herself. She will stop her incessant demands as soon as she realizes that you will no longer respond to unreasonable requests. Put a thermos of water or juice next to her bed so she can pour her own drinks. If she has a fever, give her the amount of liquid she must drink each hour and tell her you'll be back with refills when the hour is up.

Let her be responsible for her own entertainment and activities. Early in the morning ask her what books, toys, and games she would like for the day and put them in an "entertainment carton" near the bed. Leave a pencil and paper by the bed and tell her to write down any additional requests for the entertainment carton. You can fill these requests when you bring more liquids.

It's okay to spend some extra time with your daughter but do this when it is convenient for you, not when she is demand ing company. It helps if she knows ahead of time when you will be spending time with her so she can look forward to it. Don't plan to spend too much time with her, however. You want to ease the boredom of recuperation without providing an attractive payoff for being sick.

As soon as possible allow your daughter to resume personal and household responsibilities.

Dreading the Doctor

Q. My children are afraid to go to the doctor's office. When they get vaccinations or other injections they make a big fuss and embarrass me. How can I change their attitudes about going to the doctor's office and keep them calm when they are going to get a shot?

A. Fear and pain are parts of life that all people, kids and adults, are periodically faced with. To try to protect a child from such feelings is impossible and unnecessary. Children need to learn to accept their feelings of fear and pain and to express them openly and appropriately.

Children learn to accept and express these emotions and experiences when adults allow them to do so without interference. Often an adult will mistakenly try to reassure a child that his pain is nonexistent and his fear is babyish. Let's face it, getting a shot does hurt. So be honest with your child. Say to him, "I can see you are afraid of going to the doctor because the shot will hurt. You are right, it will hurt for a few moments." This way you acknowledge the child's fear and he knows it is okay to feel this way. You also teach him that the pain is temporary.

It can be helpful to give the child an activity to concentrate on that will divert him from the needle going into his skin. Try letting him squeeze one of your fingers. Or recite a nursery rhyme together. When the shot is over, ask him how long the pain lasted so he learns to recognize how temporary the pain is.

When the visit to the doctor is over, encourage the child by commenting on his increased ability to handle the experience. A child's self-confidence is boosted every time he realizes he has successfully handled a difficult situation.

It Ain't Fair!

Q. My son is constantly complaining that life is unfair. Each day he comes home from school with a long list of injustices supposedly committed by friends and teachers against him. I feel sorry for him; he seems so miserable much of the time. Last year I even insisted the school change his classroom but he came home with just as many stories of unfairness from his new classroom. How do I cope with this situation?

A. Realize first that all things in life are not fair. All things are not as we would like them to be. Fairness is often defined as sameness, and there is no way life is the same for everyone.

In every school and in every classroom there is always a child who manages to be "picked on" by the others. As miserable as the child may seem, there are payoffs to being picked on. One payoff is the extra attention the child receives from

---

Give Complete Attention When your child is talking to you about concerns important to him, give him your full attention. Often busy parents listen with half an ear while continuing to do another activity. Your child will not feel that he has been completely understood unless you give your full attention to what he is saying.

everyone, kids and adults alike, although the attention is negative. And if the adult feels sorry enough for the child, the adult will often try to make things better by changing the child's school environment for him or by giving the child "treats" to make him feel better.

To cope with this situation, first understand that it is not the parents' job to solve all of life's problems for their child. If you try to do this, even if you are motivated by genuine love and caring, the message you will be giving your child is that he is not capable of handling problems himself. Dealing with the problems and injustices in life is part of growing up.

The next time your child comes home with his complaints, give very little attention to his stories. Reflect his feelings back to him with a statement like "You really seem upset about that." Ask some clarifying questions about what he is going to do about his problem. Avoid giving advice about what you think he should do. Don't spend more than a few minutes discussing the injustices of his day. Instead, turn the conversation around to deal with the positive experiences that occurred. Ask him what part of the day he liked best or have him tell you about a learning activity he thought was really exciting. Spend at least twice as long discussing the positive experiences. In this way, you'll minimize the payoffs for your son's complaints about life.

"I Hate You!"

Q. When my daughter is very angry she often screams "I hate you" at me. When I tell her it's wrong to talk that way to a parent, she gets even more upset and threatens to run away. Is there an easy way out of this situation?

A. The way out is not necessarily easy, for it involves a change of behavior on your part. Realize that anger is an emotion we use to change another person's behavior. My guess is that when this situation occurs you and your daughter are in a power struggle. You want her to do something; she wants to do something else. Or perhaps she has asked for something and you have said no. In either case, she tries to manipulate you into changing your mind by showing you her anger and screaming unkind words.

The way out of a power struggle for a parent is to refuse to fight. Take the wind out of a child's sails by refraining from getting angry yourself. Realize that when a child says "I hate you" it does not mean there must be hatred underlying your relationship. The statement is a powerful way of manipulating a parent to give in to a child's demands. Usually this sentence translates to mean "I don't like it when I can't have my own way." What your child hopes to get from saying "I hate you" is a parent who says *yes* when *no* is more appropriate.

Respond calmly to such a statement with words like *Oh*, or *Tell me more about it*, or *I'm interested in your feelings* or *You're pretty mad at me, huh?* This will let the child know that you are willing to listen but that you can't be manipulated by angry, unkind words. When faced with a calm parent who refuses to engage in a power struggle, a child is free to choose more cooperative behaviors.

You're Okay, Whether You Win or Lose

Q. Our only child, a six-year-old son, brags unmercifully to his playmates. When he wins a game he always shouts, "I won, I won," about six times or until he gets a response from his friend, who is already quite aware at the end of the game who the winner is. Also, he is a poor loser. Midway through the game, if it appears that he'll lose he doesn't want to finish the game. How can we help him change this disturbing behavior?

A. Your son equates winning with being okay and losing with being not okay. When he brags about winning he is attempting to hold to the okay feelings as long as possible, by keeping the focus on what he sees as his success. When he quits he is attempting to avoid the not okay feelings that he experiences when he loses. He gets these not okay feelings because he confuses his value as a person with his perform ance.

When his performance is less than perfect he sees himself having less value as a person. Make sure that neither Mom nor Dad is modeling overly competitive behaviors, behaviors that put too much stress on the importance of winning. Then, to help your son change these behaviors, work to change the attitudes that confuse his self-esteem with his performance. He needs to hear certain basic messages about how to live in the world.

- You're okay even if you don't win.
- We love you just the same whether you win or lose.
- It is more important to play and enjoy doing things than to win.

He needs to hear these messages often directed either at him or at other members of the family so that the ideas become part of his life and he can base his actions on them. He'll hear these messages most clearly when he is not engaged in his bragging or quitting behaviors.

The motivation behind the bragging, the attempt to feel okay about himself, actually is a good one to foster. It should, however, be expressed in a more acceptable manner. It should not be expressed toward a person who has just lost, in a way that says "I'm better than you."

Tell him to save comments about his success for family members. Take some time at the dinner table each day to let each family member brag by relating one or two successes experienced during the day. This will change his bragging from boasts and putdowns to a legitimate and healthy means of feeling okay about himself.

Minimize Mistakes

Q. My nine-year-old son doesn't like to make mistakes. Whenever he loses a game such as cards or baseball he sulks and complains and sometimes even cries. In school when there is a competitive activity like a spelling bee, he's very unhappy if he makes a mistake and doesn't win. I keep telling him that it's okay to make a mistake and that he shouldn't get so upset, but it doesn't seem to help. What else can I do?

A. First, don't feel sorry for him. An essential part of growing up is learning to deal with frustrated desires. Parents often try to shield their kids from life's frustrations. Don't. In your child's case, he desires to win but doesn't. Let him experience his unhappiness and tears. Don't involve yourself emotionally. Instead, let him talk about his feelings and let him know that his feelings and tears are okay.

It sounds as if your son is a perfectionist and that his self-concept is based on how well he performs different activities. Let him know that you love and care for him just as he is, whether he is first or not, whether he makes mistakes or not. Show him the mistakes that others in the family make, parents included. In fact, it's good dinner-time conversation to talk about mistakes made during the day. It is important to include what people learned from their mistakes and what plans they are making to do things differently in the future. When mistakes are discussed in such matter-of-fact fashion they become less frightening. This will help your child to learn that his self-worth is not tied to winning and to perfect performance.

Faking and Fibbing

Q. My daughter likes to tell me stories about things that happen that I just cannot believe are really true. Yet when she does something wrong she readily admits it, so I don't think she is really a terrible liar at heart. Why does she make up these stories and how can I stop her?

A. Making up stories is very common among young children, especially those children who are read to a great deal. It is an early sign of intelligence and imagination. Preschoolers will often present fabricated stories as reality. At this young age the distinction between fact and fiction between what they wish had happened and what actually did happen—is not yet clear.

By six or seven years of age this dividing line should be in focus. If it is not, it could be an indication of the child's fear that she won't be noticed or receive adequate attention unless she embellishes the truth.

To correct this behavior, sit down with your child and make up an embellished story of your own. Afterward, explain that the story was make-believe and then tell her the real story. Ask her to do the same about something that happened in her world, first tell an embellished story and then tell the real story. After you have done this a few times, whenever your child begins another story, ask if it is going to be real or make-believe. After a while, the make-believe stories should decrease.

If you find your child insisting that an obviously made-up story is a real one, don't argue the matter, just calmly state that you enjoyed listening but that it sounded like a make-believe story to you. If you argue it will only force her to loudly defend her position.

Don't discourage her further by calling her a liar or telling her that she is a "bad girl" because she makes up stories. Realize that telling tales is the behavior of a child discouraged about her own feelings of worth and belonging, who needs as much support and encouragement as you can give her.

No Hurting Allowed

Q. We have three daughters, ages six, four, and one. The problem is that our six-year-old always wants to pick up the baby, sometimes to the point of hurting her. I have tried reasoning with her, punishing her, separating the two, giving extra attention, ignoring the situation and even allowing her to help more with the baby. Nothing works. I'm sure it's jealousy but I don't know what else to do. I'm afraid to leave them alone for fear the baby will be hurt. Can you give me some advice?

A. Keep up two of the things you are already doing. Continue to give the six-year-old extra attention and let her help care for the baby. When a child misbehaves it is a signal that she is not feeling secure about her place in the family and this extra attention and involvement with you will help increase her security and sense of belonging.

Some evening when you have time to spend alone with your six-year-old and everyone is in a happy mood, sit down with her and explain that all of us have mixed feelings toward the other members in a family. Sometimes we like a sister and sometimes we don't. Sometimes we feel glad that Mommy and Daddy had another baby, sometimes we feel angry because the baby seems to get more attention than we do. Let her know she is loved even when she feels this way. She is not a "bad" girl because she has "bad" feelings. Feelings are not good or bad, they just are. Tell her its okay for her to express these feelings to you at any time.

However, be very clear that you will allow only the verbal expression of these feelings, that she will not be allowed to act hurtfully toward her sister, by picking her up, or in any other way. Give her a doll or stuffed animal or pillow that she is allowed to act hurtfully toward instead of hurting her sister.

Encourage her to verbalize her negative feelings while acting negatively toward the doll. Do this with her a few times, so she sees it's okay because Mommy is playing with the doll in the same way. Keep emphasizing the difference between having feelings and actually hurting another person.

Next, establish a plan of action you will follow if she hurts her sister in the future. Tell her she will be given a choice either to stop hurting the baby or go to her room or some other place in the house where she will be separated from the baby. Tell

---

Baby Beware of calling the youngest child in the family "baby," whether the child is two, twelve, or twenty. Kids who are called "baby" often use the name as a license to act in a babyish manner, making unreasonable demands for undue attention or unnecessary service from other family members.

---

her it is her choice, indicated by how she decides to behave, whether she stays or goes. Then carry through by seeing that she leaves the room or is removed whenever the harmful behavior appears. Say nothing at these times; action is all that is required at the moment of conflict. Be as consistent as you can about carrying through with the agreed-upon plan.

Another way to help your daughter understand her ambivalent feelings toward the new baby is to read together some of the excellent books on the subject in the children's section of your local library.

Wiping Away Tears

Q. I get upset when my daughter, age eleven, cries. I know it is good for kids to be able to express their feelings, so why does it bother me so much?

A. You are right. One of the most healthy, supportive things a parent can do for a child is to allow her to express a full range of emotions. Yet when it comes to sadness and tears, it can cause a great deal of anxiety for the parent. This anxiety stems from some false beliefs parents have about childhood and parental roles.

One such is belief in the "happy childhood." Parents with this belief feel that kids shouldn't have to experience "real life" with its frustrations and unpleasantness at their young age.

That false belief in a happy childhood is often coupled with the erroneous idea that anything your kids experience and feel is a reflection of your success and worth as a parent, and that other people will judge you to be a poor parent if your child experiences sadness.

Another cause of your anxiety might be the idea that somehow you caused the tears and unhappiness. If you were a better parent, all-knowing and all-caring, and able to be a perfect parent in all respects, the unhappiness wouldn't occur.

Realize that when your child cries you don't have to somehow, magically, take away the hurt and make things sunny again; but you can sit close to the child, perhaps with an arm around her shoulder, and listen to whatever is on her mind. You let her know she is loved and cared for by your closeness and listening and that you respect her right to have these emotions.

Constant "I Can'ts"

Q. Our son, age twelve, appears to lack self-confidence. He is forever saying "I can't." His school grades are average and the teachers tell us he could do much better if he'd just try harder. What causes this lack of self-confidence?

A. A number of factors can combine to produce a lack of self-confidence. Probably the strongest factor is the fear of making a mistake. In our society adults often point out the things a child does wrong much more quickly and frequently than the things a child does right. Fault-finding and frequent criticism discourage a child's belief in his own abilities.

A factor related to the fear of making mistakes is the need to be perfect. The child decides that nothing short of 100 percent accuracy is acceptable. This is discouraging because such perfection is rarely achieved. Kids frequently give up instead of attempting or completing a task at a less than perfect level.

Sometimes it isn't perfection that kids fear they can't reach, but rather an exalted image of someone else's attainments. This happens when adults compare their kids to other people, especially to brothers and sisters. When a child decides that there isn't any way he can meet the expectations, that he will not be like this other person, he gives up.

Overprotection also lowers a child's self-confidence. When a parent does something for a child that the child could do for himself, the message transmitted to the child is that he is not capable of doing it. After many similar experiences the child starts believing the message and becomes discouraged about his own abilities.

No amount of talking about how the child "should" feel more self-confidence will help. Instead of talking, take action. Stop noticing mistakes, criticizing, comparing, and overprotecting your child. Comment on all the things your child does well even if it is just a part of the task and not the end result. Give attention to any improvement shown. Give positive recognition for specific strengths and talents. Recite often the history of your child's successes. Treat your child as if you believe him to be the most capable person in the world and eventually he'll believe it himself.

Fight in the Open

Q. My wife and I are arguers. We feel it's better to put conflicts in the open and hash them out than to always go around smiling and pretending the problems don't exist. One issue we can't seem to resolve, however, is whether or not we should argue in front of the children. Does it hurt kids to see parents arguing?

A. On the contrary, it is very helpful for kids to see that not only are disagreements a part of living together but also disagreements can be discussed and resolved. It is better to do this out in the open than behind closed doors.

Obviously, it's not good for your kids to witness name-calling, mudslinging battles. But those aren't good for anybody.

Kids usually know when parents are fighting in secret, and if this happens frequently they can become confused and scared. They wonder whether they somehow are to blame for the fights or whether one parent will be hurt or whether a separation or divorce is pending. Because the parents are not fighting out in the open the kids are afraid to talk about these feelings, which makes the feelings even scarier.

So when you disagree, don't leave the room or shut the door. Explain to your kids that it is okay for moms and dads to disagree and argue with each other and that the arguments lead to solutions of problems. Tell them it does not mean that Mom and Dad don't love each other, or that they are going to get a divorce, but that it simply means they are working out problems.

Once you have said this to your kids and argued a few times in front of them, you'll probably find that they become very matter-of-fact about the whole thing and will disappear anyway when you start to argue. Watching other people argue is a very boring pastime!

She's Playing "Yes, but . . ."

Q. My daughter frequently says she is bored and has nothing to do, yet she turns down all of my suggestions. Help!

A. Your daughter has you playing a game called "Yes, but . . ." She asks for advice, you give it, then she turns down each suggestion. The longer the game continues, the more frustrated each of you becomes.

It is not a parent's duty to constantly provide amusements for a child of any age.

Your daughter is not looking for suggestions but is really interested in getting your attention, in keeping you busy with her. Make a mental note to give her plenty of attention at another time during the day, not when she is seeking it through game playing.

King or Queen for a Day　Add some extra holidays to your calendar this year. Designate one day per child when Mom or Dad will give exclusive attention to that child. The child and the parent will plan the day together, the only restrictions being distance and the parent's pocketbook.

When you give your child your undivided attention in an activity either in or out of the home, you are giving something far more valuable than any material gift. Children two and three years old are not too young to appreciate the specialness of this day, nor are teen-agers too old.

You can teach your child not to play "Yes, but . . ." in a number of ways. When she pretends she has nothing to do, sit at the kitchen table, put your head in your hands, and say, "I'm thinking." After a couple of minutes of watching mother "think" your daughter will become disinterested and will find her own amusements. A second way to handle the situation is to invite your daughter to help you make a list of all the household chores that need doing. Watch how quickly she finds something else to do.

Kids' Plays Shock Parents

Q.　Recently our three kids got together with some of the kids in the neighborhood and made up a series of plays. I don't know about the other parents but I was shocked at the content of some of these plays. Imagine seeing a seven-year-old walking around with a Pepsi bottle filled with water and pretending to be drunk! Another little girl took a handful of M&M's for a headache. Whenever any character in the play had an argument with another it always ended with one person shooting the other. Where do such young children pick up these ideas? Do you think that what they playact now is an indication of what the kids will be like when they grow up?

A. Young children, in their imaginative play, model the world they see in their homes, their neighborhoods, and on television. Unfortunately, it's often not a pretty world that they see. It is very important for us to become aware of the messages kids receive from the media about alcohol, drugs, and violence as parts of everyday life and try to counteract these messages.

We need to be careful, too, that the messages we give our kids verbally match the messages they get from our behavior. If Mom or Dad reaches for alcohol to relax or to liven up a party, the kids are likely to copy this behavior when they get older. If our medicine chests are filled with rows of bottles for every imaginable symptom, the kids will learn that relief is only a pill away, never mind the cause. If kids see violence, either physical or verbal, being used to solve family problems, they'll have a tendency to do the same.

Just the fact that your kids made up one play showing drugs, alcohol, and violence doesn't mean they'll necessarily

---

It's What You Do, Not What You Say It has been said that kids follow in the footsteps that the parents thought they had covered up. In other words, kids model their behavior on what they see parents and other adults doing, not on what these adults tell them about proper behavior.

Kids are keen observers and clearly notice when parents exhibit behavior that they have labeled undesirable. An example of this is smoking. If you smoke, all the lectures in the world your kids hear on the dangers of smoking will make less impression on them than the fact that they see you smoking. So, if you notice behavior in your kids that you feel is undesirable, look to see if anyone in the family is teaching that behavior to the kids through adult modeling. You just might decide to change a behavior of your own in hopes of convincing your kids to do the same.

have these problems as adults. But the play can stimulate you to think about how you will teach them other values.

Accidents Downplay the emotional scenes that often accompany childhood accidents. Attend calmly and rationally to the medical needs of the situation. The message you want to give to the child is: "I can handle this accident and so can you."

Acknowledge that tears and expressions of hurt are okay and appropriate to the situation and temporary in nature. When all has been taken care of, give your child a kiss or hug and let everyone return to what they were doing before the accident occurred.

Childhood accidents are part of life. If treated in a calm, matter-of-fact way, they don't get blown out of proportion and the child doesn't receive the unnecessary service and attention that might lead him or her to become accident-prone in the future.

Bumps and Bruises Keep frozen ice packs handy in the freezer for all the little emergencies that keep cropping up. The easiest way to make an ice pack is to wet a small kitchen sponge, place the sponge inside a plastic bag, then twist and seal the bag. The packs will keep indefinitely in the freezer and are reusable.

Running Away Sooner or later almost every child reaches a point when he announces he is going to run away. This announcement might be made in anger during the heat of an argument or in disgust after a series of discouraging events. It is a declaration of independence on the part of the child, who means to shock, anger and hurt the parent.

A parent's most effective reaction is to remain as calm and objective as possible. Don't demand that the child stay at home; don't ridicule his feelings; don't predict disaster if he leaves. Ask calmly what his plans are, how he will live, and what his forwarding address will be. Some parents even offer, in a friendly way, to help the child pack!

Running-away episodes handled in this manner usually are short-lived. When your child returns, allow him to save face. No "I told you so." Just a hug and an "I'm glad you're back" will suffice.

Moodiness Parents need to accept the fact that their kids will sometimes seem out of sorts, moody, or disagreeable. These emotions are a part of life, for kids as well as adults. It's unrealistic to think kids will always be happy and cheerful.

Teens are particularly susceptible to moodiness and quick swings of emotions. When you see your child like this, don't get upset or artificially try to cheer him up. Let him know you are available to talk if he wishes to share what's on his mind.

If you find your child too grumpy to be around, it's easier to move to another spot in the house than to remove the kid. Be careful your kids don't get the impression that their moodiness upsets you, or moodiness will become a tool they can use whenever they want to upset you.

Bike Safety One of the ways to impress upon children the need for good bike safety habits is to clip all the newspaper articles of bicycle accidents for the kids to read. Though the articles may be gruesome and scary for children to read, they will bring home clearly and strongly the dangers inherent in bicycle riding on public streets. This does not mean that riding bicycles shouldn't be permitted but that if children do ride, good safety habits are a must.

Expose Your Mistakes One way to teach your child not to fear making mistakes is to admit your own mistakes. Let your children see that no one is perfect, that mistakes are a part of learning how to live. Share with your children your plans to do something different in order to avoid the same mistake in the future. In this way you teach the kids to learn from their mistakes and to have the courage to be imperfect.

> **Dr. Rudolf Dreikurs Said It** "It's not so important that you made a mistake. It's what you do afterwards to improve on the situation that counts."

What Would You Do If . . . ? Teach your children to solve problems by sharpening their abilities to think of different responses to difficult situations that might come up in their lives. Play the game of "what would you do if . . . ?" with them. Set up hypothetical situations like "What would you do if your teacher blames you for something you didn't do?" or "What would you do if your friend urged you to take something from a store without paying for it?" It's good that family members of all ages brainstorm possible responses, for the younger children can benefit from the experience of older siblings when information is being freely exchanged.

"What would you do if . . . ?" teaches your kids that there are usually many different responses to a given situation, not just the one or two responses that quickly come to mind. It also prepares them with viable responses in case the situations do arise.

Saying No A child has to be told no occasionally. Knowing how to say no effectively when your young child behaves unacceptably is a valuable skill for parents. It is important to make clear what a child may not do and why. It's just as important to give the child an alternative behavior which is acceptable. For example, you might tell a child crayoning on the walls: "You may not crayon on the walls because it leaves marks that won't come off. You may crayon in your coloring books or on paper." Another example: "You may not jump on the couch because jumping destroys the material and the springs. You may jump in the yard or down in the basement." In other words, you are taking an unacceptable behavior and teaching your child that behavior that is not okay in some places is acceptable in other places. A good rule of thumb is to give two yeses for every no, or two ways that are acceptable for the child to continue the behavior.

Points to Remember

It is normal and healthy for a child to experience the full range of positive and negative emotions.

It is normal and healthy for a child to be faced with unpleasant, frustrating experiences from time to time.

The job of parents is to support and teach their children to cope with unpleasant experiences, not to shield their children from them.

Allow everyone in the family, adults included, to make mistakes, to feel okay about these mistakes, and to learn from these mistakes.

It's okay to say no when appropriate and to set unpleasant consequences for misbehavior.

8

●●●

Money Matters

As parents we must make many decisions about money matters that concern our children. We must decide on the best system for giving money to our kids, whether we will pay them for chores or give them a fixed allowance or just hand them money when they make reasonable requests. If we do decide to give the kids an allowance, how much should it be? What expenses should it cover? What should we do when they want something their allowance won't cover? If they don't do their chores, should we withhold the money?

Today, with rampant inflation and money so tight, we wonder how to teach kids the value of the dollar. How can we teach them to appreciate how hard we work for the money we earn? How do we teach them to tailor their requests for material things to fit our budgets? How can we teach kids to plan and budget and save?

We must also decide just how much of the family financial situation our children should know. There is probably no other aspect of family life that is guarded as secretly as the family finances. Salaries, budgets, major spending decisions, taxes, and insurance are rarely discussed by the family. In a two-parent family, often one spouse doesn't even know exactly what the other earns. We need to decide how much of this information to share with our kids.

Reasonable Expectations

The first experience your child will have with money is spending it. The five-year-old who buys a candy bar for 35¢ has learned that nickels and dimes in his hand can be exchanged for something he wants. You can expect the spending decisions of young children to be capricious, impulsive, and erratic. They'd much rather splurge than save. Saving money has little value for the five-year-old—he prefers to spend it as quickly as possible for something he wants. As the child grows, you can expect his spending decisions to be a little more deliberate. However, even by age twelve this spending behavior may not be fully mature, and he may frequently use poor judgment. Don't be alarmed, that's all part of the learning process.

By age twelve, the child can be expected to begin budgeting his money. Money for fixed expenses such as lunches, bus fare, and scouts will have to be set aside before all is spent. Again, while your child's performance in budgeting will show improvement during the years from five to twelve, it will still be erratic and imperfect at twelve. So you can reasonably expect occasional pleas for help, for handouts, or for loans from a kid who is out of money when a crucial need appears. Your child's ability to save some money to meet such unexpected needs will also begin to develop during these years.

If your child has been on a consistent allowance system, by age twelve he will probably experience the need for extra money. To earn the extra money, your child may ask to do additional household chores, over and above the normal everyday chores, for a fee, perform odd jobs for a neighbor, or even go out and get a newspaper route. Great!

Making Allowances

Q. We are having disagreements concerning allowances at our house. I think allowances should be tied to chores, so that the kids receive a set amount of money for doing specific jobs. If the kids goof off and don't do their chores, they get no allowance. I figure this way the kids will learn the relationship between working and earning money. My wife thinks kids should get a weekly allowance regardless of the work they do around the house. Who is right?

A. Both of you are right to a certain extent. Let's look at your wife's argument first.

The best way to teach children the skills of managing money is to provide them with an allowance structure that gives them a limited amount of money on a regular basis. At first this allowance can be just a small amount of spending money. By the time a child reaches age eight, he is old enough to be responsible for buying some necessities and having slightly more spending money. You can gradually increase the intervals of time between allowances from one week to two weeks to a month as your child becomes more adept at budgeting and saving.

The amount of money you give your child depends on his age, his experience and ability in handling money, the cost of the necessities that the allowance must cover, and your economic situation. However, one rule of thumb is to start small and increase the amount gradually. Be sure to have a clear agreement concerning exactly what necessities the allowance is expected to cover.

The basic allowance should not be tied to everyday

household chores and responsibilities. Since parents are not paid for performing general chores around the house, children should not be paid for similar work.

Every member of the family needs to experience both the privileges and duties of being part of the family group. One of the privileges is receiving a sum of money, however small, to be used for personal wants and needs. One of the duties is household chores, a duty in which all family members share without payment.

Payment for general chores teaches kids that they must always "get something" for everything they do. If a child does not perform his chores properly, it is more effective to let the child experience a consequence that is related to the chore than to withhold his allowance.

Now let's look at your argument. Children must somehow be taught the relationship between jobs and money. As they grow older, they find that their allowance doesn't cover all their expenses. They find that if they want to have enough money, they need another source of income. Now is the time they can best learn the relationship between working and earning money.

Since it is not realistic to expect most youngsters under sixteen to find paying jobs in the open market, it is appropriate for parents to pay kids for performing jobs that are not considered routine household chores. Any chore that parents routinely pay someone else to do can be done by a willing child for pay. A child may ask to wash the car, for example, and be paid the same amount that is paid at a car wash. Or a child may perform extra cleaning tasks, such as washing windows or waxing floors, for an agreed-upon sum. One parent I know pays 25¢ per pair to have his shoes polished by his kids. When you allow even a very young child the chance to work to earn money you establish a sense of independence and self-reliance early in life.

Cents Slip Away

Q. I have an eight-year-old who squanders money. I work hard for the money I give him and it burns me up to see him run to the store every time he has a cent, to spend it on some toy that doesn't last anyway. I have decided not to give him any more money until he becomes more responsible and learns the value of money. Am I justified in not letting him have any money of his own until he has learned to spend it wisely?

A. I can understand why it would bother you to see money wasted today when most families really have to pinch and plan to make their money cover all necessities. A desire to help your child learn the value of money and become responsible in his spending habits is also understandable. However, your decision to withhold money from him and make the spending decisions yourself will not teach him to be responsible with cash.

If children are to learn the value of money, they must be allowed to handle money, allowed to make both wise and foolish decisions on how to spend it, and allowed to experience the consequences of these spending decisions. You cannot expect them to learn to handle money responsibly before they've had experience spending it.

An effective way to teach your child the value of money is to make it available to him in limited supply. Strangely enough, most kids see the money supply as inexhaustible. They know that if they ask, complain, whine, or throw tantrums they can often get money out of Mom or Dad, or certainly out of Grandma or Grandpa. They wheedle and cajole to try to convince you that what they want to buy is justified. Sometimes you give in, sometimes you don't. But their tactics work just often enough that the kids decide that money is available if they learn just how and when to ask for it.

The best way to teach kids that the money supply is exhaustible is to put them on a regular weekly or monthly allowance and stick to it. Make it clear that they can count on just this much and no more. When this is spent they will not get any more until their allowance is due again, no matter how they ask or beg. No advances or handouts. A few poor spending decisions that leave them without any spending money for a while will be powerful lessons toward learning to spend wisely and carefully.

A Tale of Wasted Dollars

Q. Our daughter, age ten, saved a long time to buy a toy she saw advertised on TV. She had the toy only a few weeks before the parts began to wear out. There was no guarantee with the toy, and the store where she bought it refused to take it back. She is very upset. How can we make her feel better about what happened? Do you think we should replace the toy for her? It really wasn't a very good buy in the first place, but she refused to listen to us when we tried to tell her so.

A. Hard as it may seem to a young child who has saved her pennies, there is a good lesson in this sad tale. The consequence of buying a poorly constructed toy is that it breaks quickly. You will destroy her chances of learning this lesson if you replace the broken toy.

From this experience a child can learn a great deal. She can learn to examine a purchase ahead of time, to see if it looks like it will break easily. She can ask her parents or the salesperson questions about the toy's construction. She can also learn to ask about guarantees and return policies before she buys something in the future.

Sometimes a broken toy is not only a matter of poor buying judgment. Often it is defective merchandise or shoddy workmanship. The manufacturer should know about it. And the consumer, your daughter, should let him know.

Suggest to your daughter that she write a note with her address and an explanation of what happened, enclose it with the entire broken toy, and mail it back to the manufacturer. The address and zip code are usually on the box or the toy. Mark it "first class mail enclosed" and have her ask for a replacement or a refund. Learning to do something constructive about an experience that upsets her is a valuable experience for your daughter.

To Lend or Not to Lend

Q. Should we lend our youngster money? Sometimes she spends all of her allowance early in the week. Then something special comes up over the weekend that she wants to do with some friends, but she doesn't have enough money. I'm uncomfortable about lending her the money, but I also don't want her to miss out on the weekend fun. What do you suggest?

A. I suggest that if you want to teach her to be irresponsible with money, you should advance her next week's allowance whenever she asks for it. She will quickly learn that it's okay not to plan ahead and save, because Mom and Dad will give her what she needs if she runs short.

If you want to teach her to budget wisely and carefully, tell her the next time you give her the allowance that you are not in the banking business and therefore cannot give out loans. Tell her that you are confident that she is old enough and smart enough to budget wisely. The hard part will be the follow-through. The Saturday night will come when her friends head for the movie and she is excluded because she is broke. She might pout, cry, or call you unfair. Don't scold or remind her that it was her fault that she spent all of her money. Let her know you understand how miserable she feels staying home, and express hope that another week she might decide to spend her money differently.

Saving School Lunch Money

Q. I give my children enough allowance to cover the cost of school lunches. Recently one of my boys decided that he'd come out ahead by making sandwiches for himself and pocketing the lunch money for other things he'd rather have than a hot lunch. Seems to me this system is costing me double. I pay for both the school lunches and the sandwich fixings. Should I subtract the lunch money from his allowance if he continues to fix sandwiches?

A. If you do, he'll probably go back to buying lunches since there will be no incentive to make his own. What you need is a solution that encourages his initiative to earn extra money yet doesn't cost you more.

There is a solution that accomplishes both of these goals. Ask your son to decide at the beginning of each week, or whenever he gets his allowance, how many days he will buy lunch and how many days he will make his own. A look at the school lunch calendar, usually available in the local newspaper a week ahead of time, will help with this decision. Then offer him half the amount that school lunch costs for each day that he makes his own. The difference should cover your costs, and he'll have some extra spending money that he wouldn't have if he bought lunches every day.

A word of caution: make sure that he understands that he is expected to take full responsibility for cleaning up when he prepares his lunch in the kitchen.

School Savings

Q. I give my daughter a fairly generous allowance, and expect her to save 50¢ each week. Her school has a banking program which will handle such small transactions. I have told her that if she doesn't save 50¢ per week, I will reduce her allowance. I'm willing to let her have the extra money to teach her to save but am not willing to let her have it to squander. She complains I am unfair. Do you think so?

A. The issue is not really one of fairness. The issue really is: will enforced savings teach your daughter good saving habits? The answer is: not necessarily. There are more effective ways to encourage these habits.

One fact of life many parents hate to accept is that parental lectures and pressures do not necessarily influence children's beliefs and attitudes. What does influence them is the example we set. You can increase the mileage you get out of setting a good example if you add the following two steps:

1. Let your daughter see you exhibiting the desired behavior as clearly as possible. In this case, take her to the bank with you when you make deposits or show her how you do it by mail. Be sure she notices when interest is added to your account. If you use different types of savings, such as money market accounts, stocks, or bonds, explain these in as much detail as is appropriate to her age. Explain why you are saving and what you expect to do with the savings. Don't add the pressure words "and you should do it, too." Just let her see your example clearly.
2. Show the tangible benefits of saving. When you do cash in savings for a purchase or a vacation, let her know it. Or when the proverbial rainy day comes, large or small, explain how the money you needed was ready and waiting.

When you force your daughter to save a certain amount each week, you teach her only to comply with your pressure. She will not necessarily learn the merits of saving. Indeed, such forced compliance at one age may lead her to react by displaying the opposite behavior at another age.

Who Should Pay the Library Fine?

Q. My kids are not very reliable about returning books to the library on time. The library frequently sends me notices that fines are due. The kids say I should pay the fine because I don't give them much of an allowance. Are they right?

A. No, they are wrong. If they borrow a book from the library they take on the responsibility to return the book on time. The consequence of not carrying through with this responsibility belongs to the kids. In this case, the consequence is paying the fine.

The kids should pay these fines with their own money. If they have no savings and receive a small allowance, they can work to earn the money. There are always extra household duties beyond the routine chores for which they can earn enough to pay off their fines.

You Break It, You Pay for It

Q. While playing at a friend's house yesterday afternoon, our nine-year-old son accidentally broke a lamp in the living room. His friend's mother handed him a dust pan and broom and asked him to clean up the mess. Then she called us to tell us what had happened. Should my husband and I offer to pay for the damages our son did? Since it was an accident, not really his fault, I'm not sure we need to do anything more. What do you think?

A. Accidents are unfortunate, but since your son broke the lamp, regardless of how it happened, he really should be the one to pay for the damages. That way he will learn the relationship between his actions and the consequences of his actions. He will learn responsibility for his deeds, whether planned or accidental.

Most likely at age nine he will not have enough allowance to cover the cost of the lamp. At today's prices, it would probably take him so long to earn and save the money that the entire affair will be too discouraging to be a good lesson for him. At this point I recommend you go into partnership with your child. Let him pay back a portion of the cost of the lamp while you make up the difference. Figure out the amount he should pay by comparing the cost of the lamp with the amount of allowance and savings he could reasonably be expected to contribute. Then make his share a little higher so he will have to do some extra jobs for you, or even, perhaps, for his friend's parents, to earn enough money to complete his contribution.

Don't Do Son's Job for Him

Q. My eleven-year-old son has taken on a paper route for the first time, and it has caused endless problems for my wife and me. Sometimes he has an activity that keeps him late after school. On these days he asks his mother to pick up the papers for him. When it rains he asks her to drive him on his route. On weekends, when delivery is in the morning instead of the afternoon, he oversleeps unless I drag him out of bed.

I don't want him to lose the route and I do want to encourage him to earn money for himself, but I get aggravated when I have to get so involved with his job. Is a father expected to do all this to help out his son?

A. No! Your involvement is actually teaching your son to be irresponsible and inconsiderate. If he learns these traits now, chances are he'll behave the same way in later jobs.

Have a talk with him some evening soon when there has been no problem with the paper route and both of you are in calm, relaxed moods.

Begin by expressing your delight that he is working and is mature enough to earn money for his needs. Then explain how important you feel it is for him to handle the route independently. State clearly that you will no longer pick up his papers when he has an activity; he will have to make choices about how he uses his time and will have to solve this problem for himself. The same goes for rainy weather. Ask him if he has sufficient rain gear to handle the rainy days. See that he has an alarm clock for weekends and state that you will no longer wake him up to see that he gets out on time.

Don't let him suck you into thinking it's a parent's responsibility to do these things. He may become upset and angry with you. After all, he's had a good deal up until now, with the major responsibility for the job falling on your shoulders. He won't willingly give that up. However, state calmly that the route is his job and you have every confidence that he can handle it effectively. If the responsibilities seem too much for him, suggest that he go into partnership with a friend.

Let Them Balance the Books

Q. My wife and I have very little of our paychecks left after paying for necessities. Yet our kids want us to buy everything they see advertised on TV. How can I help my children understand the value of money?

A. Kids don't often have a clear idea of family finances, so it is no surprise that they think Mom and Dad can afford to buy much more than is possible. If you want your kids to understand the value of money and understand how much a paycheck can buy, give the kids a lesson in family finance. This lesson can take two different formats depending upon the ages of your children. If you have elementary-school-age children at home, cash your paychecks, sit around the table with the kids, and let them help you divide the money into the necessary piles for meeting the family's expenses. Make separate piles for food, rent, clothing, gasoline, heating fuel, telephone, savings, and so forth. No words will make as much impact on the kids as actually seeing how little money is often left after the necessities are taken care of.

If you have older children at home, you can show the same financial breakdown with pencil and paper. You can give the older kids the responsibility of writing the checks for family expenses. Mom or Dad will sign the checks, of course. Let the kids sharpen their math skills by balancing the checkbook. Once they have an understanding of the family financial picture, they will be much more cooperative about living within the budget boundaries.

Teach Money Management

Q. Once a month my husband and I pay bills, balance our checkbooks, and budget our money for the following month. How much of this should we share with our children? Is it important for kids to know the details of the family finances?

A. One of the best ways for parents to teach their kids about money is to involve them in all aspects of family finances from the time they are old enough to go to elementary school. Strange how secretive most people are about their money, how much they earn, how much they save, how they budget. Yet kids can only come to appreciate the value of the dollar if they see how money is used in the real world. Kids can be taught that information about the family's finances is private and is not to be discussed outside the home.

Kids need to know how much money different members of the family earn. It's part of their career education to know how much people earn in different occupations. They need to see how that money is budgeted and saved and spent. They need to know about taxes and insurance.

You can involve children in family finances in two ways: by letting them participate in discussions about the family finances, and by letting them participate in the actual transactions with money.

Discussions about family finances occur when decisions need to be made. How much should we save each month?

Where shall we go on vacation this year and how much will it cost? Can we afford a new TV? Discuss options, alternatives, consequences of the decisions with your kids. Solicit their opinions. They don't necessarily need to have a vote in the final decision since their knowledge of finances is not that sophisticated. They will appreciate being part of the decision-making process.

Kids can participate in cash transactions at stores and banks; they can fill out checks for parents to sign, and depending upon their math skills, can help balance the checkbook. The more financial procedures they actually take part in, the better they'll understand the world of money.

An added benefit is that kids who are aware of the family resources and the difficulties their parents face in making ends meet are much less inclined to make excessive demands for clothes or items that would fracture the budget. Cooperation comes with knowledge.

Points to Remember

Don't link allowances to chores; don't withhold money for uncompleted chores. Do not use money as a reward or punishment.

Be consistent with the allowance structure. Resist pleas for extra handouts. Don't give money in place of love, attention, or to assuage guilt feelings. Remember, you're not in the loan business.

Mind your own business about kid's spending. They should have complete freedom over how to spend their money. No lectures, no criticizing. Allow the kids to make spending mistakes and to learn from them without your interference.

Encourage your child's efforts to supplement his allowance by working. All outside work commitments must be fulfilled by the child, not the parents.

Involve your kids in family financial affairs.

9

• •

Dealing with Divorce and Remarriage

My kids, your kids, our kids—what hassles can arise within a family when loyalties are confused and divided because of a divorce and remarriage.

Kid to stepmother:

"You can't tell me to clean my room. You're not my *real* mother."

Kid to divorced mother:

"I like it better at Daddy's house. He gives me presents each time I come and never asks me to help with the dishes."

Kid to divorced father:

"I'm lonely here. I miss my mother and my friends. I want to go home."

Kid to remarried mother:

"Mom, John [the stepfather] won't stop his kids from picking on me. Why do his kids have to come and visit us anyway? Can't you send them home?"

Kid to remarried father:

"How come I have to do chores and her kids don't? You're not being *fair.*"

Raising kids today is hard. Divorce and remarriage add a whole bunch of extra problems to this task, problems many parents didn't expect and don't know how to handle.

Reasonable Expectations

There are two things you can expect to have to deal with when you divorce and remarry: unpleasant feelings and instant chaos.

Expect divorce to be a time of sadness, a time of loss, a time of change. There is no way to make it a happy time for children, even if the parents were at war with each other and the separation makes good sense for all concerned. You can expect your kids to be unhappy when one parent moves out and the family is broken up. Expect them to be confused about the change and have many questions about it. It is reasonable to expect, and essential to allow, the expression of all feelings, questions, and concerns. You cannot expect quick change and instant adjustment from your kids. The process of grieving for the lost family and getting used to the new arrangements will take time, most likely a year or two. Don't expect the process to go faster.

Remarriage is often another time of loss for the children, so don't expect them to automatically share your feelings of delight and happiness. There are many changes that come with remarriage that may upset a child, perhaps a move, perhaps new kids sharing the house, perhaps a loss of parental attention as someone new begins to take up Mom's or Dad's time. There's also the loss of the dream that many children of divorce hold onto—the dream of the parents getting back together again. So it's not unusual for the kids to express resentment and displeasure at this time.

If you are a new stepparent you can't expect to establish a strong relationship with each stepchild quickly. According to Dr. Emily Visher and Dr. John Visher, founders of the Step-family Association of America, it takes about a year and a half for a strong parent/child relationship to develop. The process can't be rushed.

You can expect a great deal of chaos early in a remarriage: visiting kids, divided loyalties, differing routines in the household to be merged, rules and responsibilities to be sorted out. And there is no time for the new couple to be alone together, to cement their relationship before having to deal with children on a day-to-day basis.

With time, patience, understanding, careful planning, and coping with the specific problems that arise, you can expect your children to weather divorce and/or remarriage and even perhaps come out stronger for it. There's a sense of satisfaction and mastery that comes when one of life's most difficult situations has been encountered and everyone is okay at the end.

When and How to Tell the Children

Q. My husband and I plan to separate shortly. So far, we have not said anything about this to the children. When should we tell them? Also, how should we tell them? Together, or one at a time? I'd like to make this as easy as possible for my kids.

A. Parents can minimize the unpleasant effects of a separation on their kids if they follow some basic guidelines. Notice that I said minimize, not eliminate. No matter how well you handle the separation with respect to your kids, you must expect and allow them to express anger, sadness, confusion, and anxiety. These feelings are normal and appropriate to the situation and must be dealt with before the kids can accept and adjust to the situation.

Tell your children as soon as your decision to separate is

final. Don't put your children through the confusion and pain of an on-again/off-again separation. They will lose their confidence and trust in you. Keep the period between the time they are told and the time the physical separation occurs short. The waiting period before a parent moves out is extremely hard on everyone. Emotions are raw, everyone is edgy, flare-ups occur all too easily. The kids need a week or two when both parents are still in the same house so that all of their questions can be answered. The worse way to separate is for one parent to secretly move out and let the other parent tell the children. Such a situation often leaves a child with the fear that one day he will come home from school and the other parent will be gone too.

It's helpful if both parents tell the children together. Then there's much less chance for one parent to become the "bad guy." It also makes both parents available to answer questions.

Tell all of your children at the same time, no matter what the span in ages. You want the kids to find out directly from you, not from a brother or sister. Being together helps solidify feelings of support and closeness among the children. Older kids can help younger ones understand. There'll be plenty of time during the next few days to spend alone with each child answering questions.

State the reasons for the divorce as honestly as you can, touching on all of the major issues involved, no matter how unpleasant. Dealing with known issues is always easier than dealing with the fantasies one conjures up when the truth is hidden. You do not need to give personal and private details of either parent's life. Don't make light of the seriousness of the reasons or your kids will become confused about the need for the separation. If only one parent wants the divorce the kids need to know this. It is not a fact that can be covered up easily. The children will lose respect for the honesty of both parents if they sense they are not being told the truth.

It is essential that your children get the following messages loudly and clearly when you tell them about the separation:

- Parents may divorce each other but they do not divorce their kids.
- Divorced parents have just as much love for each of their children as married parents do.
- Children are in no way to blame for the divorce.
- The separation is a decision made by the parents and there is no way for the children to bring their parents back together again.

Be sure to tell your children whatever you know about the living and custody arrangements that will be made so they can anticipate and prepare for the changes to come.

Dos and Don'ts for Weekend Dads

Q. I am a divorced father. My kids visit me every Sunday from 10 A.M. until 4 P.M. Once a month they come on Saturday, sleep over for two nights, and I take them to school on Monday morning. I enjoy being with them but am running out of interesting ways to entertain them. Frankly, I am sick of Sunday afternoon movies, the zoo, the park, and the local fast-food restaurants. Any suggestions?

Parental Independence   The other day a very perceptive single father of a ten-year-old son told me that he realized early in his son's life that he had a choice. He could either devote 100 percent of his time to raising his son and give up all of his own freedom and independence, or he could raise the boy to be independent so that both could live lives of their own. Every parent is entitled to a life of his or her own; the kids do not need to occupy every hour. A parent needs interests, friends, and activities that he or she enjoys. Parents who deny themselves the freedom to be a complete person often smother their kids with too much attention and raise dependent kids. In the end, both parents and kids feel resentful.

A. It is not necessary to provide fancy entertainment each time your kids come for a visit. By doing so you provide them with an unreal picture of what Dad's divorced life is like. You may also provide an unhappy comparison between the weekend time spent with Dad and weekday life with Mom. There's no way a mother can compete with a divorced dad who entertains the kids royally once a week while she asks them to pick up after themselves, do their homework, and eat leftovers.

It is very important for a child to experience the normal, everyday life of the noncustodial parent. Let your children participate in the ordinary routine of your life. Cook together, do laundry, clean house, shop for groceries, and so forth. The time spent doing these activities together allows plenty of opportunities to talk together and to share the activities that occurred during the week while everyone was separated. It's much easier and more natural to talk and share when a parent and child work on a task together than when a parent and child sit down at a hamburger joint and Dad self-consciously says, "Okay, son, tell me all that's happened this week."

The visitation schedule that you have established has enough time for occasional outings. Perhaps during the long weekend you share each month, one trip could be planned. Let the children help plan these outings with you. You might find that you have overlooked some obvious places that they would like to visit such as the local library, an art museum, or even the home of a relative of yours. These trips can be fun for all as long as they occupy only a small portion of the weekly visitation time.

Visiting Kids Make Messes

Q. I am a divorced father. When my two children come for their weekend visits they leave my house a mess. Toys and clothes are everywhere. I don't want to nag and punish them because I'm afraid they won't want to visit me so much if I do. Can you help?

A. Yes. There are two problems here: the mess itself and your fears that the children will not want to visit you if you punish them.

You have a right to expect your kids to pick up after themselves even if they are very young. Be sure they have a permanent place to keep toys and clothing while they are visiting. The place doesn't have to be fancy, a drawer or a box in the closet is sufficient. Also, be very specific with them about where certain activities can occur. You might want to limit toys to the bedroom floor and the kitchen table. Schedule regular clean-up times each day, including a time shortly before they are to leave at the end of the weekend. While they are picking up their items, use that time to pick up things of your own. That way you are modeling the behavior you want the children to learn.

A "pick-up box" is another handy idea. Get a barrel or big box, the type major appliances come in and put it in the garage or basement or a closet. Explain to the children that when you find toys and clothes in places where they don't belong you will put them in the box. In some families kids have to wait a day before retrieving anything from the pick-up box. In other families kids have to do an extra chore before retrieving an item. You might give the kids the responsibility of putting items you leave in the wrong places into the pick-up box too, as children are more cooperative in families where the rules apply equally to all members.

It is true, as you fear, that nagging and punishing will discourage and alienate your children. Learn to discipline more effectively through establishing routines such as clean-up times and consequences such as pick-up boxes. That way the children will learn responsible behavior, will enjoy the visits, and the house will stay clean.

Differing Routines

Q. My ex-wife called me the other day and asked me to follow the same routines she follows with the kids when they come to visit me. That means the same bedtimes, the same responses to misbehavior, the same chores. I really don't like this idea. One of the issues that separated us was a disagreement over how we should discipline the children. Will it hurt the kids if, when they are in my home, I do things differently than their mother does?

A. We underestimate the ability of kids to adjust to different living arrangements when we insist that everyone treat them exactly the same. They do have the ability to understand and to react appropriately to two homes that are run differently, without this harming them in any way. Keep the following guidelines:

1. Each home should have a clear, consistent set of routines and consequences for misbehavior. Both homes need structure, though the structure needn't be exactly the same in each home. It is important for kids with two homes not to view one parent as the taskmaster and the other as the permissive good guy who allows anything and everything.
2. Each parent should be allowed to take charge of his own relationship with the child. The parent the child is with should be totally responsible for the child's behavior. If difficulties do arise, each parent must learn to deal quickly and appropriately with the problem in his or her own fashion.

    When parents follow these guidelines, they are free to establish a home life with their kids that feels comfortable to them and will prevent the kids from playing one parent off against the other.

I'd Rather Stay Home

Q. My seven-year-old daughter doesn't like to visit her father on the days she is supposed to go, though I'm not sure why not. If I force her to go, won't it do more harm than good?

A. Any child who has the opportunity should be encouraged to maintain communication with both parents after a divorce. It's important for your daughter to keep in contact with her father. You'll need to talk with her about her reluctance to visit, to see if she's aware of what's bothering her. Do this in the middle of the week, not just before she's supposed to visit. You'll also need to talk over the situation with her father, so he doesn't build up anxiety and resentment towards his daugther. He may be able to offer solutions to the problem, too. There are several possible conditions that may contribute to her reluctance to visit.

- She feels strange and confused about being in a new place.
- She is lonely for her neighborhood playmates.
- She dislikes being used as a messenger between Mom and Dad.
- One or both parents question her excessively about the other parent's private life.
- One or both parents criticize and downgrade the other parent, trying to force her to take sides in continuing disputes.
- You express feelings of loneliness when she's gone. She feels guilty for having "caused" your unhappiness.

If any one of the above conditions is part of your situation, take steps to correct it. The strangeness of the new place will pass with time, especially if much of her visit with her dad is spent at his house rather than out running around. If she's lonely, occasionally let her take a friend when she goes visiting. You may also suggest to her dad that he frequently invite one or two of the neighborhood children over to play so she can find new friends. If either parent is using her as a messenger, informant, or ally against the absent parent, *stop immediately.* When you or your husband force your daughter to take these roles, you hurt her badly. It's okay to let your daughter know that she is missed but reassure her that you'll be just fine alone, that you're glad she is going, and you hope she has a good time.

Visits with a parent should be handled just like going to school. One is simply expected to go. The older the child grows, the more flexible the schedules need to become to accommodate the other interests of the child; but don't ever let the visiting stop completely.

If the situation persists, or your daughter's reluctance increases, family counseling is needed. A child's relationship to each parent is too important to be allowed to weaken or stop completely.

Which Parent Enforces the Rules?

Q. Who should discipline the children in a stepfamily, the biological parent or the stepparent? My wife and I disagree on this one. She tells me I should discipline her kids because I'm a man and she thinks they will listen to me better than they listen to her. But when I do discipline them she usually criticizes me afterward for how I handled things. I think she should discipline them. After all, she is their mother. I don't want to seem like the heavy all the time. Who is right?

A. It would help if you and your wife stop fighting and criticizing each other and take a different approach to this problem. Discipline should not be an arbitrary matter, with the parent who is present deciding on the spur of the moment how to punish a kid for doing something wrong. Your stepfamily should spend many evenings talking about rules and routines, defining acceptable and unacceptable behavior. Make very clear decisions and post charts that remind everyone what is expected.

Spend time as a group deciding on consequences for violations of the rules or displays of inappropriate behavior. When these discipline policies are established in advance everyone will know what's expected and there won't be any surprises. There will be much less chance that your kids will feel that you are unfair or playing favorites. You'll avoid the complaint of "But Mom (Dad) let's me do that!"

In a stepfamily, at least in the beginning, it is best if it is the biological parent who enforces consequences as needed. It will be more accepted by the child because there is already an established bond between the parent and the child. The new stepparent needs time to build a close, trusting relationship with the child before doing too much disciplining. He or she does this by concentrating on the nurturing role of parents, while the biological parent has both the nurturing and disciplining roles.

However, for times when the biological parent will not be present and a situation will need to be handled in his or her absence, it is good for the biological parent to transfer the authority to enforce consequences to the other parent in front of the children. Say something like, "I'm going out for the evening. Your stepfather is in charge while I'm away." Say this often in a new stepfamily. As time goes on the kids will get the idea without the verbal acknowledgment.

There is one type of situation, however, not covered by the above guidelines. In problems that occur strictly between the stepparent and the child, such as a child using a stepdad's tools and not putting them away, it is best if the other parent doesn't get involved. A stepparent should handle any such situations by him or herself, without being criticized by his or her spouse.

"You're Not Good Enough for My Dad"

Q. My new husband's eleven-year-old daughter Marcia arrived recently to spend the summer months with us. I have only been with Marcia a couple of times, as this is a fairly recent marriage and she lives in another state. I can already tell she doesn't like me very much. Yesterday at the dinner table she blurted out, "You're not good enough for my dad." I've been bending over backward to be kind to her but she obviously doesn't appreciate my efforts. What do I do next?

A. First you will have to change your own expectations of how she should feel about you. This visiting arrangement may be more difficult for her than it is for you. Your marriage might mean an end to her fantasies about Mom and Dad getting back together and she may blame you for that. Or she may view you as a threat to her dad's attention to her. She may feel that if she likes you she is somehow disloyal to her own mom. So refuse to take her statement of rejection personally. It doesn't necessarily mean that you have failed to win her over. It more likely means that she is going through a difficult period of adjustment which will require a large measure of acceptance and understanding on your part. It is not necessary for her to experience and express warm feelings for you right away.

A word of caution, however. It is important for you and your new husband to agree not to let her feelings interfere with your relationship. Your husband needs to say clearly to his daughter that although he would be pleased if the two of you form a close relationship, his marriage to you will remain close and strong with or without her approval of you.

Next, learn to listen calmly when she vents her feelings. Tell her that her feelings are okay. Do not pressure her to change them or try to convince her with logic that you really are good enough for her dad. And be careful not to strike back at her verbally with criticisms, putdowns, or sarcasm. If you have other children, be careful not to treat her differently than you treat them.

Do involve her in family activities from which, with time and patience, warm feelings can blossom between you.

Stay out of Stepchildren's Squabbles

Q. Ours is a blended family. I have two daughters by a previous marriage and my husband has a son and daughter from his first marriage. We have all been living together for almost two years now and frankly I had thought that by this time our household would run a lot smoother than it does. The kids squabble a lot and are constantly running to us with complaints about each other. Even more infuriating are their accusations that we are both unfair, that we favor our "own" kids in settling arguments and don't care for all the kids equally. We do try to be fair in settling disputes but at times we really can't tell who is at fault. We try so hard to be fair that sometimes it seems almost as if we favor the other spouse's kid. How can we get the members of this blended family to operate as one close family?

A. Armed with some insights into how the kids are using the blended family situation to manipulate you, you will be able to see how the advice I give to all parents to stay out of the kids' squabbles also applies to your situation.

Kids learn marvelous ways of manipulating parents and getting their own way. In your family they do it with words. *Fairness* to them means "do it my way; give in to me; let me have what I want." They probably entrap you with phrases like "You treat your own kids better than me" or "You can't tell me what to do. You're not my real mother (father)." Then, due to the guilty feeling that you're not doing a good parenting job, you give in.

Once you realize that their words are being used for manipulation, it will be much easier for you not to fall into the trap. You don't even have to answer the accusations when they are thrown. It is not necessary to explain and defend yourself over and over again.

It is especially important for parents of blended families to have the faith in their children that they can all learn to live together in relative harmony. The best way they can learn this is for the parents to stay out of the squabbles and allow the kids to learn the skills of settling problems by themselves.

Picking on Younger Stepbrothers and Stepsisters

Q. I recently married a man with two teen-age boys. I have eight-year-old twins, a boy and a girl. I'm forever having to dry the twins' tears after one of the older kids has hurt them. How can you get teen-agers to stop picking on stepbrothers and stepsisters that are much younger?

A. It's all too easy to blame the older children when fighting starts between brothers and sisters. We figure if they'd just lay off, leave the little ones alone, all would be peaceful. But would it? Let's look at the role the little kids play in starting a fight, and the payoffs they receive for getting older siblings to fight with them.

Young kids have dozens of different ways they can drive an older brother or sister up the wall. They can annoy by chattering constantly, interrupting, messing with another's belongings, or muttering under their breath words guaranteed to anger. Little kids are smart. They know how their parents see the difference in relative size, so they rarely provoke an older sibling in obvious ways. Instead, they set the scene so it looks like they were just doing some innocent behavior that's relatively harmless. To the parents, it appears that mean old brother just picked on the young ones for no reason at all.

When the older sibling loses his cool the parent often cracks down and punishes him. This punishment is carried out much to the hidden glee of the younger child who has now very successfully managed not only to annoy his brother but to get him into trouble with Mom and Dad, too.

To alter this pattern, older kids need to have alternative methods for dealing with annoying younger siblings. Some evening when all is peaceful, sit down with them and discuss alternatives. Sometimes a *polite* request to stop the specific behavior will be effective; very often it's the unpleasant way older kids treat an annoying sibling that eggs the younger kid to annoy further. Or maybe they need to remove themselves from the presence of the younger child. Perhaps the annoying behavior is really the younger child's request for attention from an older sibling; five minutes of attention might be all that's needed to get rid of the unwanted behavior. Let the younger children know that they share responsibility for any fights that occur, and that you will not protect them anymore by punishing the older kids when fighting erupts. When this protection is removed, as well as the payoff of seeing their brothers get into trouble with Mom and Dad, watch how they learn not to instigate trouble!

Plan for Summer Visits

Q. My stepdaughter will be coming to spend a few weeks with us this summer. How can I help her feel at home while she's here?

A. You will need plenty of time when she first arrives for the entire family to meet and talk together. One purpose of these family meetings is to set up the routines by which the family will operate, including mealtimes, bedtime, laundry, and room clean-up procedures. Another purpose for these family meetings is to plan family outings and activities together. Let her know that you waited until she arrived to plan family fun times so that she feels that she is an important part of the family group.

Take some time to brainstorm activities for rainy days. Post the list of activities and make sure she knows where to find any items she might need for these activities.

Integrate her into the neighborhood group of children as soon as possible. Have a picnic and invite local children her age; or see if the neighborhood school has a supervised playground time with planned activities that she could join.

It is very important for her to have ample time alone with her biological parent, especially if distances are large and she doesn't frequently visit. These times can be passed talking and sharing inner thoughts and feelings while pursuing an activity that both enjoy.

If the child expresses loneliness for her other family, let her maintain visual or verbal contact with them. For a young child, a picture of the other parent and some little trinket from home can be comforting. Frequent phone calls or letters to and from home also help. Let her know that it is okay for her to talk about her life at home and about her absent parent.

Discipline her as you do other members of the family. See page 125 for tips on disciplining stepchildren.

"But Daddy (Mommy) Lets Me . . ." Divorced parent, beware of being manipulated by kids who, when you give them an appropriate no, react by telling you that the other parent would have said yes. Single parents often fall for this routine and change the no to a yes because they fear their kids won't want to be with them as much as with the other parent if they say no. Don't make a big issue of it if your kids try this manipulation. Just a short statement that: "It's different in this house" will suffice.

More Strokes from More Folks Divorced parents need not pity their children because they have a "broken home." There can be advantages to having a split family. One big advantage, that comes with time as the parents settle down after the divorce and perhaps even remarry, is that there are now two families instead of one to encourage, love, and support the kids. Kids can always use more of these encouraging strokes and the more folks in their lives the more strokes they can get.

Bedside Picture When parents are separated or divorced, children usually miss the parent with whom they do not live. You can alleviate the loneliness a bit by allowing the child to keep a photograph of the absent parent on a bedside table or desk. This is not as easy as it sounds, for many parents separate with bitter, hostile feelings and don't want to be confronted with a picture of the ex-spouse in their child's room. If this is so for you, you must learn to separate these feelings from the needs of your child to love and experience both parents. If you can't do this by yourself, seek help from a professional counselor.

Points to remember

Allow your child to express all of his unpleasant or negative feelings at the time of a divorce or remarriage.

Establish clear, consistent household routines in a new single-parent family or stepfamily.

The best gift a noncustodial parent can give his or her visiting kids is time to be together, talk together, do everyday activities together.

Don't pressure your child to adjust instantly to and accept a new stepparent.

Allow new siblings to solve problems that arise between them by themselves.

10

•••••••••••••••••••••••••••••••••••••••

School Daze

The alarm clock rings. With luck, the kids will be up soon and getting ready for school. You wait fifteen minutes and then go and see what is happening. One kid is still in bed, another is wandering around the house looking for lost shoes, a third is hurriedly finishing homework left undone the night before. Another typical day begun.

An hour later you sit with a second cup of coffee and survey the damage. One glass of milk spilled. Peanut butter smeared on the kitchen counters from hurriedly made sandwiches for lunch. Sneakers forgotten by the back door. One child walking to school in tears because he has missed the bus. And only eleven more years of this before the youngest child finishes school.

It's even worse if you have a job outside the home, in addition to the job of parenting. There's little time to wipe up the spilled milk and smeared peanut butter, to regain your composure after the kids have left if you have to dress and be off to work yourself.

When the kids come home late in the afternoon they are only too anxious to forget all about school. But there's homework to be done, and often it's a real fight to get your kids to do it. Report cards are coming soon and you want your kids to get good grades. Yet if you nag too much about homework the conversation ends with everyone in tears and the older boy threatens to quit school when he's sixteen.

If you are working and are not at home with the kids after school, again it's harder. It's not easy to supervise homework and make dinner and do all the household chores that never seem finished.

The last letter from the PTA urged parents to support their school and encourage their kids to want to learn. With everything else a parent has to do you wonder how you can motivate their learning too. What, specifically, should you be doing? How is a parent supposed to cope with school?

Reasonable Expectations

Preparing for school, going to school, and doing homework after school are all jobs that belong mainly to the kids, not the parents.

Ideally, by first-grade-age your child can get up, pick out his own clothes, dress himself, make his bed, and be at the breakfast table at a designated time. Breakfast can be a relaxed, unhurried meal, finished in time for your child to be ready to leave for school when the bus arrives. A school-age child is capable of remembering lunches, books, sneakers, homework, and so forth without your nagging and reminding. A checklist by the door can do any reminding that seems necessary.

By age six a child can choose between school lunch and a brown bag of sandwiches. When the children are six to eight years old you will have to read the school menus to them and help them decide which lunch to have. If these young kids decide to brown-bag it you will have to plan lunches together ahead of time so you can have the necessary ingredients on hand. When the kids are older have them make up a shopping list of what they need for lunches. Any kid past kindergarten who takes a homemade lunch can make the lunch himself.

You can also expect kids to be responsible for their own homework. When they first get homework you can help them schedule their time so that it's sure to be done. You can set up a small study center for each child with a desk, a good light, pencils, and so forth. Be sure it's far from the TV. Answer questions and show interest in their homework but don't take from them their responsibility for completing it.

Don't expect your child to love everything about school all the time. Many days your child will come home grumpy or upset about one thing or another. Occasionally, when the pressure gets intense, your child may express the desire to stay home or may even feign illness to escape school for a day. These are perfectly natural feelings as long as they do not occur too frequently. Few adults love every minute of their workday, so don't expect your kids to either. When problems do occur, expect and encourage your children to talk about

Private Space   Every child needs a place in the house to call his own, where he can retreat when he feels a strong need to be alone. This must be a place where other family members won't intrude. There must be a family understanding that the child will not be disturbed by other family members when he is in his private space. It isn't necessary for this private space to be an entire bedroom; perhaps just the child's bed, above or below it, can be that space. Or try a desk or a special chair. Another possibility is a large refrigerator carton which the child decorates himself and fills with pillows.

them with you. Occasionally, if something occurs at school that you don't think your child can handle, you may have to visit the school to help find solutions to the problem.

Don't expect the school to do the entire job of educating your children. Expect the school to teach the basic skills, but realize that it is up to you to provide a stimulating home environment and intellectual experiences that will encourage your child to want to learn both in and out of school.

Minimize Morning Misery

Q. School has been in session only a short while and already I have to contend with the familiar morning hassles of getting the kids ready and out the door on time. How can I avoid this morning unpleasantness?

A. Hassles on school mornings are now being experienced in millions of households across the country, so you have plenty of good company. Step one in ridding your home of these hassles is to decide which of the morning responsibilities belong to the children. When you have decided that a particular responsibility belongs to your child, you must let the child handle it in his own way without interference from Mom or Dad. I suggest that the following responsibilities belong to all children grades one to twelve:

• Getting up in the morning by themselves. (Make sure they have working alarm clocks.)
• Choosing their own clothes and dressing themselves.
• Taking care of personal hygiene needs, including clean hands, faces, and teeth.
• Remembering to take books, homework, sneakers, and lunch money to school.
• Making their own lunches if they brown-bag it.

The same responsibilities belong to kindergarten children but during the first few weeks of school parents will need to take the time for teaching the child to carry out these tasks.

What happens when kids fail to meet these responsibilities on their own? You must not nag, remind, threaten, or scold them. Instead, let the kids experience the consequences of their actions.

Set up a scheduled time for breakfast, lasting anywhere from twenty to thirty minutes. Choose a time that ends about fifteen minutes before the kids must leave the house for school. Breakfast is served to any child who arrives at the table completely washed, dressed, and ready for school. The dawdlers and complainers will find that the only thing that happens if they don't meet their morning responsibilities is that they miss breakfast. The proper response of a parent to this child is, "I sure am sorry you missed breakfast this morning. Maybe tomorrow you'll make it on time." Remember, lectures and "I told you so" are not helpful at this point. You must remain calm and friendly for consequences to be effective.

The kids won't starve if they miss a meal or two. Though their morning performance in school might suffer due to lack of proper nourishment, this is only a temporary situation. Be wary of other adults who might try to convince you that only a terrible parent would let a child go to school hungry. Experiencing a little hunger will teach your kids a very valuable lesson in living: when you blow your personal responsibilities, unpleasant consequences occur. This type of experiential learning makes a strong impression on kids.

The consequences of forgetting to take books, sneakers, and so forth are having to go through the day without these things. Parents should not make the special trip to school to bring forgotten items, since that would only teach the child that it is okay to forget things because Mom or Dad will bail him out. Having to repeat an assignment during recess because the homework sheet is on the kitchen table and sitting on the sidelines during gym because of forgotten sneakers are power-ful incentives for kids to learn the art of remembering.

You Miss the Bus, You Miss the Boat

Q. I have three children ages eight, thirteen, and fifteen. We live far away from their schools, so they must ride the bus to school each day. The bus stops a quarter of a mile from our house at 7:10 each morning. You would not believe the chaos in our house starting at about a quarter to seven. I have to remind the kids constantly to hurry up or they will miss the bus. At the last moment someone always is missing some-thing—gym shoes, lunch money, a homework paper, you name it! By the time they finally leave, even if they do manage to catch the bus, I'm a nervous wreck. If one kid has missed the bus, I have to get dressed quickly and drive him or her to school, which I resent greatly. They're old enough to be able to get themselves ready and out to the bus on time, aren't they?

A. Of course they are. Getting to school on time, whether by walking or by bus, is a responsibility that belongs to the child, not the parent. When a child doesn't fulfill a responsibility the use of natural or logical consequences is one of the most effec-tive corrective techniques. A natural consequence is a conse-quence that occurs automatically without any parental involve-ment. A logical consequence is one that requires parental involvement but is logically derived from the situation.

The natural consequences of missing the bus are (1) the kids walk to school. You, as the parent, will have to decide if walking is feasible, depending upon the age of the kids in-volved, the distance to school, and the safety hazards of the route to school. If it is feasible for your child to walk to school, don't hesitate to let that happen. (2) Walking might mean, however, that they arrive at school late. That is a problem between the children and the school. You can hope that the teachers will ask kids coming in late to make up missed work during recess or during a free period. It might be helpful to let the teachers or principal know ahead of time that your kids are having a problem catching the bus so the school will know what has happened if your child arrived late.

If it is not feasible for the kids to walk, then you need to use a logical consequence. One possibility is to let the child who has missed the bus stay home. Since it is a school day, the child must stay in his room with his school books. No TV. No playing outside. No happy times with Mom. Will the child consider staying home a treat and arrange to miss the bus frequently? If you do not make the day at home pleasant for the child you will soon find that he much prefers to be in school where the action is. A couple of boring days at home are all it takes to teach most kids to be on time for the bus.

A different logical consequence is to drive the kids to school when they have missed the bus. Figure out how much time it takes to make the trip to school and back. The kids then owe Mom or Dad the same amount of time in extra chores. You can also compute the cost of the gas involved, which today can be considerable, and ask the kids to cover this cost from their allowance.

One very creative parent devised the following logical consequence for missing the bus: Because of high gas costs, the kids are allowed a fixed number of rides per week for after-school activities, visits to friends, movies, and so forth. If the kids need a ride to school because they have missed the bus, this ride to school is subtracted from the number of rides available for the fun activities.

The purpose of using consequences, whichever form you choose, is to teach the child to shoulder the responsibility for his actions.

School Lunches

Q. I have two children in elementary school and one in junior high. My problem is lunches. The kids say the food served at the schools tastes awful, so they want to bring their own lunches. I wouldn't mind spending my time making their lunches if it weren't for the complaints that come from at least one kid each night about what I've packed. Also, the kids often forget to rinse out their thermos jars when empty, so when I go to refill the thermos in the morning, it has a sour smell. Any suggestions?

A. Your problems with lunch complaints and sour thermos bottles will end today if you turn the responsibility for making and packing school lunches over to your children. That way they can choose things they like to eat and if they end up with a food that doesn't taste so good at noon, you are not to blame. When no one will clean a sour-smelling thermos for them, it's amazing how all of a sudden kids begin to remember to do it themselves.

Keep a lunch-shopping list taped to the refrigerator or a family bulletin board where the kids can list the foods they would like you to have handy to pack for lunches. For younger children, you might set up a specific time when lunches are to be made, a time when you can be available for help as needed. It may mean setting the alarm a little earlier so that the kids have the time before school to make the lunches, or perhaps making lunch the night before. By giving the kids responsibility for their own lunches, you are taking a step forward in teaching them responsibility.

Another way to minimize the complaints and eliminate the daily messes is to hold a sandwich jamboree once a week. Since most sandwich fillings freeze well, each child can make his or her own sandwiches for the entire week in one afternoon. A frozen sandwich placed in a lunch box in the morning will be ready to eat by lunch time.

It's a good idea to have the sandwich jamboree on the same day the weekly shopping is done, so everything is very fresh when frozen. Buy several different kinds of sandwich fillings and breads. The kids can mix and match to their heart's delight. They can even use cookie cutters to cut the bread in different shapes; save the discarded crusts and pieces for bread crumbs.

Use freezer labels to mark each sandwich with the child's name and the filling.

Sick or Well?

Q. Sometimes when my daughter complains she doesn't feel well in the morning, I can't tell if she is really sick or is feigning illness in order to stay home from school. Often when I have let her stay home, by 10 A.M. she appears to be feeling fine and happily spends the rest of the day playing and watching TV. What should I do the next time she complains she's sick before school?

A. It's very difficult when a child complains of a stomach ache, tired feeling, or general weakness and doesn't want to go to school. You can't be 100 percent sure if your child really is sick when she complains of such vague, undiagnosable symptoms. Next time this happens ask your daughter to decide whether or not she is well enough to go to school. The choice is either to go to school or to stay home in bed getting well. No baking brownies with Mom or Dad. No playing around the house. A box of quiet activities next to the bed is sufficient amusement.

Be sympathetic to the discomfort of being sick but don't overdo the attention and special services. The point is to create an environment where, if your daughter is really ill, she can get well. Yet the environment is not so rewarding that being sick becomes preferred to going to school.

If your daughter announces halfway through the day that she feels better and wants to get up, tell her you are delighted with the improvement. She can get dressed and go to school for the remainder of the day, or she must remain in bed in order to continue recuperating. Express your hopes that tomorrow she'll be completely healthy and ready to return to school.

Scared of School

Q. My nine-year-old daughter simply doesn't want to go to school. She has all kinds of excuses. Stomach aches, dizzy feelings, and nausea all seem to mysteriously attack on Monday mornings. Many mornings she dawdles until the school bus leaves without her. On the worst days she stands by the kitchen table and throws a temper tantrum. We've taken her to the doctor to have her ailments checked to make sure she wasn't really sick. He called her behavior "school phobia." What causes "school phobia" and how can a parent help?

A. Many children would rather stay home than go to school. Your daughter, however, seems to have extremely strong feelings against school. These may stem from academic, social, or home problems which should be looked into.

Often the reason for school phobia lies in unmet academic needs at school. A child who falls behind in school work, or who experiences a great deal of failure becomes frustrated by the tasks to be done. A child who keeps ahead in his work and finds the learning tasks very simple may become bored and restless in school. A frustrated child needs extra help to catch up to his class; a bored child needs enrichment to keep him stimulated and occupied. If you suspect such needs might underlie your daughter's school phobia, ask the teacher to arrange for testing that will determine these needs. If these needs show up on the tests, remediation or enrichment is called for.

A child who has difficulty getting along with the other children may develop school phobia. This child may be either shy and timid, or aggressive and bullying. In either case, friendships are few and the hours in school, especially during lunch and recess, are lonely. Ask your daughter if she has friends in school, what the other children are like, whom she spends her time with at lunch and recess. If you suspect she is having problems making friends, talk it over with her teacher. The teacher can help by occasionally pairing her with another child when there is a task which they can do together. You can help by frequently inviting one or two children in whom your daughter expresses interest to your home to play after school. Some children are able to initiate friendships more easily in the safety of their own homes. The friendships can then carry over into school. Having even one friend in the class can change a child's entire attitude about going to school.

Sometimes a problem in the home is at the root of school phobia. A death in the family, an impending divorce or separation, or a move to a new area can make a child afraid to go to school because he fears what will happen at home while he is gone. This type of situation requires tremendous patience and support for the child from the parent. You will need to set aside time each evening to be alone with your child, to listen to his anxieties about the home situation, and to reassure him that you will be there at the end of every day.

Most teachers have had a lot of experience dealing with children who fear school. They need to know if your child is having such difficulties, so they can assist you in your efforts to overcome this problem.

It's Their Homework, Not Yours

Q. I am having a terrible time each evening trying to help my daughter with her homework.

Reading assignments are okay; when she has finished an assignment, we can have a nice friendly discussion about what she has read. But the math assignments are impossible. She comes to me for help, claiming she doesn't understand how to do the problems. When I try to explain them, she complains that I don't explain it clearly or that the teacher told her something different. I find myself getting louder and angrier as we go on.

Finally she ends in tears and I'm almost screaming. Yet I feel it's a parent's job to help with homework. How can I calm her down and get her to listen to my explanations and avoid this ugly scene?

A. The scene you describe probably goes on in hundreds of homes each evening across the country. The parents want only to help but fail to take certain realities of the parent/child relationship into consideration.

Parents find it difficult to be objective about their child's learning. They want their kids to catch on quickly and easily. Their own feelings of competence are threatened if they explain something and their child doesn't understand. When they have to explain something a second time, the parent's voice usually is louder with a less pleasant tone.

The child senses the parent's frustration and in turn feels threatened about his own ability to learn competently. So the parent and child start blaming one another. "Explain it more clearly," says the child. "It's your fault if I can't get my homework done." "Listen more clearly and try harder," says the parent.

This blaming and complaining continues until everyone feels rotten.

If this situation recurs in your home, take yourself out of it. A parent need not also be a math teacher. Talk to the child's teacher and see if extra help is available in school or hire a professional tutor or an older kid to teach your child.

I Can vs *IQ* A youngster's success in school is based more on his belief in his abilities than in his IQ. This feeling of "I can" is fostered by parents who allow their kids to assume responsibility, parents who are very slow to criticize. These parents give approval and praise easily for effort, improvement, and tasks well done, and are fond of predicting all kinds of successes for their child.

It is a parent's job to encourage learning, to provide a quiet place for the child to work, and to structure the family routines so a time for studying is planned each day. Teaching specific skills is not in a parent's job description. That job belongs to teachers and tutors.

Working in Workbooks at Home

Q. My eight-year-old son's teacher has given me a reading workbook to use with him at home because he is falling behind in his reading skills. The instructions in the workbook are very explicit, so I know what to do in terms of the reading activities. But I'm not sure how to make the sessions enjoyable for the both of us, so he'll want to do the extra work. Do you have any suggestions?

A. I'm glad you asked, because sometimes when parents try to teach school skills to their children the sessions end up in terrible battles. For this reason, I don't usually recommend that a parent teach skills at home, as stated in the preceding section. However, if you wish to follow through on the teacher's recommendation, try the following suggestions.

Set up a specific structure for the lessons. You will have to decide when the daily lesson will be, where you will work together, and how long the sessions will be. Let your son have input in making these decisions so he'll feel like an equal partner. When you choose a time, be careful to avoid conflicts with other activities that your son likes to do. If he has to miss a favorite TV show, you can be sure he'll sulk and do poorly in the workbook. Allow some flexibility in the schedule to avoid conflicting with unexpected events. Make a schedule and post it in a prominent place in your child's room so there's no mix-up over when the sessions will occur. Pick a place that is quiet and free from distractions caused by other family members or the TV. A space where the two of you can be alone is best. Be sure that the rest of the family understands that you are not to be interrupted when you are working together. Keep the sessions short, since your son has already had a long day at school and probably will not be able to keep his attention on additional work for too long. Watch his reactions during the sessions, and try to stop while he is still interested in what you are doing, before he becomes bored or distracted. Often a fifteen minute period is plenty.

You will need great patience when you work with your child, patience which may not come too easily to you at the end of a long day. If you have reasonable expectations about what can be accomplished, you'll sidestep a lot of frustration. It's unreasonable to expect your child to make a lot of progress quickly, to make few or no mistakes, or to learn and remember something after you have explained it just once. You have been asked to help precisely because he needs a lot of explanation and a lot of repetition. If you expect this, and do not pressure him to succeed too quickly, you will have more luck keeping your patience.

Give your child lots of positive comments. Notice every small improvement and comment favorably upon it. You needn't wait for big gains to give praise. Notice parts of things that are done correctly, even if the whole is incorrect. Allow him frequent repetitions of things he can do correctly so there'll be lots of opportunity for him to feel successful and for you to praise him.

Make the sessions as informal and full of fun as you possibly can. Home is not school, so the style of teaching can be different. Make games out of the activities in the workbook. The teacher can help you do this. Occasionally have prizes or surprises with the games. Switch roles once in a while and let your son teach you. Don't forget to make mistakes when you are the student, for this will help your son learn that mistakes are part of the learning process.

Reinforce Reading Skills

Q. My wife and I would like to help our children improve their reading skills. We are not teachers and don't really know much about how the kids are being taught to read in school. We also don't have a great deal of time to spare. Yet we'd really like to help. Can you tell us a few things we could do?

A. Children's reading skills have the best chance to improve when parents and teachers work together. Any parent who can read and who can spare fifteen minutes a day can help. Since the schools concentrate on teaching kids the process of reading, it is appropriate for parents to work with their children on the development of a positive attitude toward reading. The parents' teaching will then complement the teacher's work. The following seven steps are recommended by the "Parents as Reading Partners" program developed by the New York State Senate:

1. Turn off the television set. It can be very distracting.
2. Look at picture books and tell stories with younger children.
3. Select books to be read aloud together. Choose books that stimulate your child's intellectual capacity, which is usually higher than his reading capability.
4. Talk about a book after you read it.

5. Take your child to the public library as often as possible.
6. Let your child see you enjoying a book, magazine, or newspaper. Be a reading role model.
7. Spend at least fifteen minutes a day reading with your child.

Stimulate Their Intellect

Q. How can we get our kids to do their homework? We tried helping, reminding, nagging, threatening, withholding allowances, and unplugging the TV. Two of our boys are now in junior high and this has been going on for years! I'm not sure I can last until they graduate from junior high, let alone high school. Any suggestions?

A. Let's first look at what parents can do to help their children succeed in school because as we do this, I think the insights you seek about homework will become apparent.

There is a great deal you can do to mold appropriate attitudes toward school and to motivate your kids to learn. Create an intellectual atmosphere in your home. Have on hand all kinds of books, magazines, reference materials, educational games and toys, and so forth that stimulate intellectual curiosity. Use, share, and discuss these materials together. Establish a quiet, pleasant area for quiet pursuits and homework.

Take family educational outings. Visit libraries, museums, art galleries. Go to plays and concerts, especially those geared toward children. Afterward, be sure to discuss these outings in great detail. Talking together stimulates and motivates your child.

Exhibit the pleasures and excitement of formal learning by taking some adult education courses whenever possible. Let the kids see you studying, doing homework, being excited about learning new ideas and skills.

Show interest in your child's school and schoolwork. Join and support the PTA. Ask your children questions and discuss the areas they are studying. Be impressed by every new learning they share with you, no matter how small. Let your kids demonstrate the skills they acquire by reading aloud or performing math computations.

It is best if parents concentrate their efforts on the above activities and do not get overly involved in their kids' homework. Homework needs to be assigned, supervised, and corrected by teachers. Certainly it is okay to answer a question or spell a word or discuss an idea, but do not take on the responsibility for seeing that the homework gets done. Kids who are not doing their homework in a responsible manner need to experience consequences set by the schools and the teachers, not the parents.

It is not effective for parents to supervise homework because kids may receive too many hidden payoffs for dawdling, procrastinating, and messing around with homework assignments. What a good way to keep a parent busy with them—coaxing, reminding, even scolding!

Many kids find it all too easy to get such negative attention from a parent and this attention reinforces the unwanted behaviors. Not doing homework can also be a way that kids demonstrate their power over parents. Think how angry a kid can get his parent by sitting at a desk accomplishing nothing.

You can turn off the TV and force your child to sit at a desk, but you can't force his hand to write out the answers, as you have found through the years with your two boys. Or if a kid happens to be angry at a parent over another issue, he can get even with the parent by not doing the homework, thereby making the parent equally angry.

So, back to your original question of how to make the kids do their homework. Leave that job to the schools. Spend your time and effort stimulating their intellects and motivating them to learn.

Threats to Quit School

Q. How should I respond to my eleven-year-old daughter when she announces "I'm quitting school when I get older"?

A. Youngsters in elementary school occasionally make this statement, much to the consternation of their parents. A similar expression: "I've decided I don't want to go to college," also upsets many parents.

The usual parental response is to give a mini-lecture on the value of school and to predict terrible things for the child if he or she quits. This lecture usually falls on deaf ears. Save your words and use a different response.

When your daughter makes such a statement about quitting school she is seeking your attention. It may be that something is wrong at school that she would like to talk about, but she doesn't feel comfortable bringing up the subject. So the first few times you hear such a statement ask her how things are going and if there are any situations at school that she would like to talk about.

If she makes the comment frequently, however, it is likely that your daughter is using the comment to upset you because she knows this is an issue about which most parents care deeply. Children occasionally choose to upset their parents when they don't get their way in some conflict.

One way to help your daughter see the value of an education is to make it clear that you expect her to assume financial independence at age eighteen or at the end of high school. If she chooses to go for further education she can receive some financial support from her parents but will be expected to contribute a substantial share of the expense herself. If she chooses not to go on for further schooling, then the expectation is that she will begin to work and support herself at this time. Completely. If she continues to live at home, which I don't often recommend, then she shares the household expenses.

Don't talk about your expectation of financial independence when the original statements about quitting school are made. Choose times when the family is together and everyone is engaging in pleasant conversation. When your daughter does make these statements, ask what plans she has made to support herself. Don't pass judgments on these plans. Just ask questions that will stimulate her to think about the effectiveness of her plans. Add an encouraging phrase like "I'm sure you'll think carefully and decide what's best for you" to demonstrate your confidence in her growing abilities to make mature judgments. When a child senses parental confidence in her ability to decide things for herself it is surprising how often she will make the decision the parent hoped she would make.

The "Terrible Teacher" Blues

Q. With three boys in elementary school, invariably at least one son will complain that he doesn't like his teacher. I never know what I am supposed to say and do when this happens. I don't want my child to be miserable all year with a teacher he doesn't like, yet I'm not sure there's much I can do to help the situation. Once I tried to get the school to let my child change teachers but the principal refused. I'd like your answer now so that if the problem comes up again this year I'll be ready to handle it.

A. It's very important for parents not to overreact to a child expressing dislike for a teacher. It is unfortunate when a child doesn't like a teacher with whom he has to spend up to five hours a day but it is not a catastrophe. If you treat it as one your child will follow your lead. This hinders his ability to cope effectively with his problem.

Don't take sides. You want to be sympathetic to your child and yet supportive of the teacher at the same time. You can do this by encouraging your child to share his feelings with you. Listen to what he says but withhold any comments on your part about the teacher's capabilities and personality. If you run down the teacher in front of the child, the child may then feel justified in misbehaving or doing poor work in the classroom.

Be aware of some of the hidden reasons children express dislike for a teacher. It may be that there is a genuine personality conflict. More often, however, the child is experiencing academic frustration or a peer problem. A child in the primary grades may be experiencing separation anxiety, not wishing to leave his parents. Frequent complaints about teachers and school sometimes result in a great deal of extra parental attention for the child, which is often just what the child is looking for.

Before you decide whether to take further action, you need the facts and details. What, specifically, is bothering your child? Is it something the teacher has said or done? How often does it happen? Are any other children involved? In other words, you need to know just what you are dealing with, whether it is a vague feeling of dislike or some specific behavior of the teacher that upsets him. It may take a few days and a lot of talking to find this out. If your child can't be specific at first, ask him to observe the teacher more closely the next time he goes to school and to come home ready to tell you about it.

Sometimes the problem will disappear after a few days if you don't show too much concern about it. Other times you'll have to become more involved in finding a solution. If the complaints persist over many days or a couple of weeks or if your child gives you specific details that you feel are valid about what bothers him, then it's time to talk with the teacher. Do this by calling during the school day and making an appointment. Don't call the teacher at home when he or she is busy with personal matters.

Don't bring angry accusations about the situation to this conference. Teachers are people too, and they will often react defensively to such behavior. Be specific about the nature of your child's complaint using the details gathered from your

> **Pampered Kids** Kids who get too much service from the rest of the family, and who therefore do not learn to do things independently, generally have a hard time adjusting to kindergarten. They are the kids who sit back and wait for the teacher to give them the same special service that their families give them. When this service is not forthcoming, they often get resentful and belligerent. Avoid pampering your child by following one of the cardinal rules of parenting: Never do for a child what he can do for himself.

talks with your child. Together, search for solutions to the problem.

If the problem is a personality conflict it may not be possible to resolve it. Teachers are individuals and your child just might not like the personality of this particular teacher. The most helpful message you can give your child at this point is: "You don't have to like everyone. It might be more enjoyable for you in school if you had a teacher you liked but it's not a requirement for a successful school year." In fact, your child will learn a very valuable lesson about how to get along in the world by learning to work with a teacher he doesn't like.

Report Card Reactions

Q. What is the most helpful way for parents to react to their child's report card? Several parents I know have promised their children $1.00 for each A on the report card. Some even insist the kids pay them $1.00 for every grade that isn't A! Does this type of monetary reward motivate kids to do well?

A. Grades belong to the child not the parents. Parents should respond to grades in terms of their kid's reactions and feelings, not their own. If good grades are sought mainly to please you then poor grades can also be sought to provoke you. If parents make it clear that good grades will please them and bad grades upset them, the child then has a powerful tool he can use to either please or provoke his parents at will. An A this year can become a C, D, or F next year if your child wants to punish or get even with you for something. Stay interested in his school work and achievement, but let the pleasures of success and pains of failure belong to the child. Monetary rewards and punishments are not necessary.

With this framework in mind, how should a parent react to a poor report card? Allow the child to express all of his feelings about the grades. Just listen; don't criticize, judge, or reason with what is said. Don't let yourself predict dire future consequences for poor grades. When he is finished venting his feelings discuss plans he can make to improve his grades. The whole family can offer suggestions at this point. Write down all the suggestions for the child to think about and at a later date find out which suggestions he has decided to use during the next marking period. Then drop the subject until the next report card arrives.

Remember that it's the child's choice of improvement plans that will most affect future grades. Parents cannot, as much as they would like, force a child to study, learn, and achieve good grades.

The following verbal messages can be given frequently during the school year to build self-confidence and a positive attitude toward learning in your child:

- I know you can improve your grades if you choose to by increasing your concentration and work efforts.
- It's okay for work to be hard.
- It is okay to make mistakes and to learn by doing something over and over.
- You don't have to be perfect or the best in the class.
- You don't have to hurry and succeed all at once.
- You can take your time and set short-term goals.
- Ask us for help whenever you feel you need it.

If your child does bring home a good report card, let the child express his feelings about the grades rather than superimposing your own. Discuss with him how he managed to succeed so well and what plans he has for continued success. Predict future successes that school achievement can lead to. The motivation that stems from the pleasures of personal achievement is stronger than a dollar bribe for a good grade.

Second Grade a Second Time

Q. My son Jimmy will be repeating second grade this year, because he is having difficulty learning to read. It's hard for my husband and me to accept the fact that our son has failed in school at such an early age. Jimmy keeps saying he's stupid and can't do anything right and that's why he's being left back. How can we all feel better about his failure?

A. Parents who feel their child is a failure because he has to repeat a grade transfer this feeling of failure to the child. Some parents feel that their success as parents is measured by how well their child does in school, so when the child "fails" their own egos are threatened. The child senses that he has disappointed his parents, and then has to cope with this in addition to his own feelings of stupidity and inadequacy.

It's important for you and your son to understand that being asked to repeat a year is not a sign of total failure, nor is it absolute proof that your son is dumb and incapable of learning. Realize that all children develop according to vastly different time tables. They learn to walk, talk, and ride bicycles at very different ages. Some developmental skills come almost automatically, and some have to be practiced over and over again. Development in one area, such as the coordination needed for throwing a ball, might come early, while development in another area, such as reading, might come very late. Your son is repeating second grade because his reading skills are developing at a slower rate than those of most other children. Look at the extra year as a catch-up year rather than a repeated year due to failure.

To help your child regain his self-confidence, emphasize every area in which your son is developing at a rate more in step with his peers. Find all his strengths and express pride in them. Perhaps he is strong in other academic areas, such as handwriting or social studies. Perhaps your son is talented in art or music or athletics. Let him know all people have strengths and weaknesses by discussing these traits in people you know, or in characters from books.

Another year in second grade will ease the frustration of being asked to read material that is too difficult for him. He will be slightly older than his new peer group, and therefore has more chance to shine in other areas of the curriculum. Often older children in a classroom become leaders and models for the other children. If he has the same teacher as last year, he knows all the classroom routines and might be able to be a classroom helper while the other children learn these routines.

If you have a positive attitude and accept your child's personal rate of development, you will feel better about the situation and as a result so will he. If you emphasize your son's strengths, he will begin this extra year in second grade with much more confidence.

Successful Parent/Teacher Conferences

Q. Twice a year our children's school schedules conferences with parents. I never know what to expect from these confer-

---

Caught Ya! Raise a child's self-esteem by playing the game of "Caught ya!" The idea is to catch the child being good, and to comment on whatever it is the child is doing. Comment verbally, or write a "caught ya being good" note and put it under your child's pillow.

ences, and often come away feeling confused about the many different things the teacher has said. Could you tell me what information I should expect from a parent-teacher conference, and how I can use this information at home?

A. Parent/teacher conferences can be a very valuable part of your child's educational experience. They give you a chance to get to know the teacher, to see examples of your child's work, to hear specifically how your child is behaving and achieving, and to receive specific suggestions about how you can help at home. These conferences also provide the teacher with an opportunity to get to know your child more completely. It is helpful for the teacher to know from a parent how the child feels about school, and if the child's behavior at home is similar to his behavior in school. For a teacher, holding conferences with parents is much more time consuming than putting a grade on a report card. Yet many are willing to put in this time because the more completely they know your child, the more effectively they will be able to teach and guide him.

There are four main topics that should be covered in a parent/teacher conference: achievement, behavior, peer relationships, and self-esteem. The discussion of each topic should include a description of how the child performs in each area, any dramatic changes that have occurred recently, and suggestions for how to help at home, when appropriate.

When you discuss achievement, you will want to find out if your child is performing at his proper grade level in the basic skills. Ask what tests have been given to determine this. You should be shown samples of your child's work. Strengths and weaknesses of his performance should be pointed out to you. The teacher can tell you what specific skills he has already learned and what new ones he will be introduced to during the year. Find out if your child needs any special academic help, either at school or at home. If so, find out what the school is planning to do about it, and whether referral to any school specialists is necessary.

When you discuss behavior, you want to know what the child is like in class. Does he listen? Cooperate? Finish work on time? Goof off? Clown around? Now is a good time to compare the teacher's description of your child's behavior at school to the child's behavior at home. If there are vast differences, see if you can find reasons for them. It will help you both to understand the child better.

When you discuss peer relationships, you want a clear picture of how your child gets along with other children. Find out if your child cooperates easily with others, shares when necessary, makes friends easily. If he has difficulties in any of these areas, find out what specific plans the teacher has for helping your child to improve his relationships with his classmates, and how you can help at home. If your child has severe difficulties relating to other children, a referral to the school psychologist is in order.

Discussing your child's self-esteem is more difficult. Self-esteem is not something that can be seen directly, or measured on a test. The teacher will be able to make some guesses about how your child feels about himself by observing how he reacts to mistakes and successes, and what kinds of things he declares he can or can't do.

To keep track of all the information you will receive during the conference, you might want to bring along a list of these topics, and take notes. If there is any particular topic that the teacher does not bring up, don't hesitate to ask about it.

Accepting Psychological Services

Q. My eleven-year-old son doesn't behave well in school. For the past three years teachers have consistently complained that he doesn't listen in class, won't do what he's told, and can't get along with the other children. This year's teacher told us that she thinks our son has serious emotional problems and has asked us to sign a permission slip so the school psychologist can see him. My husband is dead set against the idea. He says it's just a phase our son is going through and that he'll outgrow it in time. I think our son needs all the help he can get right now. Why would someone be against a child getting psychological help? How can I convince my husband that such help is necessary?

A. Some parents feel intense shame and embarrassment admitting that their child needs a psychologist's help. They see such an admission as a statement of their own inadequacy as parents, proof that they so badly botched the job of raising their child that a professional is needed to make things right again.

A fear of the diagnosis often compounds this shame. For many people, the only reason to consult a psychologist is because one is "crazy." Schools use the label "emotionally disturbed," which for some parents has the same meaning as crazy.

Lastly, some parents have the idea that psychologists work by tinkering with what's inside people's heads, and that to help their child the parents will also have to have their own heads tinkered with.

Realize that there are many reasons a child might be experiencing difficulties, and that these can be unrelated to the skills and abilities of his parents. While it is true that parents do have a large influence over their child's development, the child is also influenced by relatives, neighborhood, peers, school, and the media. Realize also that psychologists consider most of their clients ordinary, normal people who are experiencing problems that get in the way of day-to-day successful living. *Crazy* is a word rarely used today.

School psychologists usually provide evaluations, not treatment. When you give permission for a psychological evaluation, you can expect a diagnosis of what your son's problem is, and some suggested courses of action to relieve the problem. The suggestions might include doing nothing and waiting it out, changing the school program, using more effective parenting skills, or referring your child to a Mental Health or Family Service Agency for short or long term therapy.

Discuss these ideas with your husband, as they might alleviate some of his unspoken concerns. Because it's such an emotionally charged issue, it might be helpful to have an objective third person discuss it with you. Perhaps a minister or a trusted family friend would be willing to help.

Keep in mind that when dealing with a child's behavioral or emotional problems, ignorance is not bliss. The more you know about the problem and the possible solutions, the better equipped you are to help your child. The earlier a child who needs help receives help, the easier it is to make the necessary changes.

Ask the Kids　You can help your children develop good verbal and reasoning skills by asking their opinions about as wide a variety of topics as possible. Learn to ask questions about what the kids are observing, feeling, and thinking. Listen to their responses and question further when appropriate.

If you disagree, don't try to impose your opinions on them. Hold back tendencies to criticize or moralize or pass judgments. The kids will stop expressing themselves if they feel you don't accept what they have to say.

When you listen to your children's opinions you not only improve their ability to express themselves but also give them the message that you care about what they think.

Pencil Puppets　Does your child get upset about mistakes made on written homework? The fear of failure is so strong in some kids that they often get very upset and teary when they make written mistakes. Sometimes instead of getting upset they withdraw and simply refuse to do the written work.

You can often get around this problem in an elementary-school-age child by buying or making little puppets that fit on the ends of their pencils. Give each puppet a name. Make homework a game in which the puppet, not the child, is doing the written work. Give any hints for improvement or instruction to the puppet, not directly to the child.

This technique works because any blame for failure over mistakes the child makes is transferred to the puppet.

Hint: Send a couple of extra puppets to school with your child.

Lunch Boxes Does it surprise you how many lunch boxes a child can manage to lose during the school months? One way to cut down on this is to include the cost of buying a lunch box in the child's allowance. Let the child select the box, pay for it, and mark it clearly with his or her name. Children tend to be much more careful with items they have paid for. If the box is lost anyway, then it's time for a brown bag until the child has saved enough to replace the box. It is not a parent's responsibility to replace things a child loses. When parents constantly replace lost items they deny the child a chance to learn the responsibility for his or her own belongings through experiencing the consequences of losing them.

Lunch Notes Kids who take lunch from home really enjoy finding an encouragement note from Mom or Dad tucked in with the sandwiches. No need to make the notes lengthy. A funny picture, an "I miss you" statement, or a word about a forthcoming evening activity is sufficient. If the lunch box is a paper bag, you can make the picture or write the note on the bag itself.

Points to Remember

Getting ready for school and arriving on time is a responsibility that belongs to the kids.

Homework is to be done by the kids, not the parents. Homework should be corrected by the teacher, not the parent. Consequences for failure to do homework should come from the school, not the home.

It is the parents' job to provide an intellectually stimulating home environment for their children.

Bribes for good grades are not the strongest motivation for school achievement.

Don't badmouth your child's school. When problems arise, gather all the necessary information, talk with the teachers and administrators until you find an acceptable solution.

11

●●●●●●●●●●●●●●●●●●●●●●●●●●●●●●●●●

Victory over Vacation

"Yippee. School's out. No more teachers, no more books . . ." Whether it's two days for Thanksgiving, two weeks for Christmas or two months for the summer, the kids are jumping with joy. Vacation time has finally, finally come again.

Look in any school building around three o'clock on the last day before vacation and you'll see the teachers looking as happy as the kids, even if they do appear somewhat exhausted.

Look at the parents waiting in the schoolyard or at home for their youngsters and you will find the only group of people who are not overjoyed that another vacation is about to begin. They wonder if they have the strength to get through yet another school vacation. Many parents remember all too well previous vacations during which the kids wanted snacks and goodies all day long, left messes all over the house, complained of boredom, and demanded entertainment when they ran out of things to do. The TV set blared all day; kids fought with each other. They refused to do their normal chores because they were "on vacation," which to them meant time off from all responsibilities.

Perhaps these same parents are also remembering the difficulties they encountered the last time they took their kids on a vacation trip and are wondering how these difficulties can be avoided on this year's trip. They may even be hoping to find a way to make the coming trip educational as well as entertaining.

Reasonable Expectations

Parents can expect the kids' vacations from school to be pleasant times for the entire family, not just the kids. Parents won't have to listen for early morning alarm clocks, watch the last minute frantic dash for the school bus, soothe frustrations over homework at night. When released from these daily pressures the family should be able to relax and enjoy a change of daily routine.

Yes, the daily routine will change during vacations, but don't let routines disappear entirely or chaos will descend upon your home. It is reasonable to expect kids on vacation to follow routines regarding meals, chores, TV watching. Being on vacation is no excuse for not taking care of household responsibilities. In fact, additional routines and chores may have to be added during vacations because of the extra hours the kids are home and the different activities, such as swimming, they may engage in.

You can expect kids on vacation to provide most of their own entertainment. Nowhere in your parent's license does it say that the job of being a parent includes entertaining kids who can't find anything to do. As children grow up they should learn to fill their time constructively without constant help from Mom or Dad. A taste of boredom motivates a child to find interesting things to do on his own. Don't rob your child of this growth experience by assuming the responsibility for filling up his time during vacations.

Vacation times can also be the time for pleasant family trips. You can expect kids to behave well on trips if you carefully plan the day's schedule and activities to accommodate the kids' needs. With planning, these trips can benefit your child educationally as well.

Plan in Advance

Q. I need some help in coping with school vacations. When kids are home for a couple of weeks we all seem to get on each other's nerves. The kids like to sit and watch TV for five or six hours a day, which I refuse to allow. When I shut off the tube they complain that they have nothing to do. Then they start fighting with each other. If I try to relax by myself for a few minutes in the middle of the day, undoubtedly one of the kids will disturb me by tattling about a brother or a sister. How can I make vacation time pleasant for all of us?

A. Advance planning is the key to a pleasant vacation with your kids. While adults often prefer unstructured vacation days, kids fare much better with routines and structure. There are four basic areas of family life that need advance planning: daily living routines, TV watching, parent-child activity times, and independent activity times.

The daily living routines include mealtimes, clean-ups, and household chores. During vacations, keep these routines as close to their school-year schedule as possible, thereby avoiding the disorganization that occurs when living routines are interrupted.

Control TV watching by advance planning and scheduling what shows will be watched. Sit down as a family when the weekly schedule appears in the newspaper and choose the shows to be watched during the week. Post the schedule on or near the TV. Make some buttered popcorn and enjoy some of the specials with the kids. Encourage them to discuss the shows with you afterward.

During vacations plan special parent-child activities that require more time than you usually have available during the school year. These activities might center around a new hobby that all ages in the family can enjoy, such as bread baking or making candles. Perhaps your family would enjoy a music hour together each night, the content of which can be chosen by each family member in turn. A wide variety of records can be borrowed from most local libraries. Another fun family activity is reading plays together, with each person in the family taking different parts. Again, most libraries have books and magazines of plays written for kids. Let your kids know the time of day these activities will occur so they won't constantly nag you to do them.

To plan independent activity times for your kids, gather the family together and list all the activities kids can do on their own. Post this list in a prominent spot. Tell the kids that when they have nothing to do they can consult the list to find an activity that appeals to them instead of coming to you.

With these advance plans to guide you, enjoy the vacation!

Routines When School Is Out

Q. Having kids home all day makes me feel like I'm running a hotel. The children eat snacks and meals all day long. No one wants to help around the house because they say they are "on vacation." They constantly nag me to drive them to the park, to the swimming pool, or to a friend's house. I do want them to enjoy the summer, but each year by the end of July I'm not sure that I'll make it through August. Can you help me get out of the hotel business?

A. The only way to put order and sanity back into your life is to develop consistent household routines for the summer months.

First, let's look at the meal situation. If you have young children and you do all of the food preparation, schedule the times when breakfast, lunch, and dinner will be served. You might also want to schedule morning, afternoon, and evening snack times. Children do not need to eat more than six times a day. For those who become thirsty between meals and snacks, water is a great thirst quencher. Set out plastic cups and leave a pitcher with ice on a low shelf in the refrigerator or on the back porch. Give a child who is too young to tell time a page with clock faces drawn upon it that shows the eating times. Even a young child can recognize when the drawings match the kitchen clock. That will prevent innumerable queries of "Is it time to eat yet?"

You could decide to allow older children to take certain meals and snacks whenever they want, providing they clean up completely when they are finished. Failure to clean up properly should result in the loss of the privilege.

Second, you must be deaf to the kids' arguments that because they are on vacation they don't need to work around the house. As long as they enjoy the benefit of the household, the food and the shelter and the love of the family, they need to contribute their share of the effort needed to make the household run. The easiest way to assure their help is to schedule a "family work time" right after breakfast, before any fun activities begin. That means before TV, playing outside, going swimming with friends, and so forth. This is known as Grandma's Law: *First we work, then we play.* You will have to decide how long the family work time needs to be by comparing the number and ages of your children to the amount of work that's necessary to keep the household running smoothly. If you have kids who dawdle, schedule the work by jobs finished rather than minutes worked.

Once the work gets done and the meals are no longer a hassle, you will be able to enjoy the park, the pool, and other summer activities with the kids without feeling like an overworked hotel manager.

Siblings Aren't Sitters

Q. I am eight, going into third grade. In the summer my mom makes me take my little brother everywhere I go. He sure is a pest! Can you tell me what to do about it?

A. It is reasonable for your parents to ask you to spend some time each day with your little brother, especially at a time when Mom or Dad has other responsibilities and really needs this extra help. This is one way you can make a worthwhile contribution to your family. Your little brother then has a special time to be with you and to learn by doing things with you. He enjoys this because you seem so grown-up and competent to him. Yet your brother also needs to learn to amuse himself for much of the time.

When parents put an older child in charge of entertaining a younger brother or sister for long periods of time they are making a mistake, a mistake which breeds resentment on all sides and interferes with good family relationships. Here's why.

The older child feels resentful because she is burdened with child-care duties that really belong to the parents. The parents feel angry when the older child doesn't willingly assume these duties, and the younger child is robbed of an important part of growing up, which is to discover how to amuse himself.

In addition, the younger child learns from this situation that he can manipulate people. If he wants big sister to do something with him that she does not want to do he has only to complain to Mom or Dad. The parent then forces the older child to do what the younger wants. The older sister takes out her anger and resentment at being manipulated on her younger brother, which makes him feel bad. So everybody loses.

Vacation Tripping

Q. Each year our family spends some vacation time traveling by car. Some trips are long and require two or three days in the car. Others require only a few hours in the car each way. Regardless of the amount of time we spend traveling in the car, my three kids manage to fight and annoy my husband and me constantly. They get bored, tired, restless, and hungry. They fight over who is stuck in the middle of the back seat and who will sit on which side of the car. Is it too much to hope that kids can actually behave in the car?

A. Kids can be taught to behave in the car and can even travel cross-country successfully. The secret to success is that old Boy Scout motto—Be Prepared.

Hours spent in the car can be divided between quiet, individual times during which each child is expected to amuse himself and family times during which everyone can participate in an activity.

To prepare each child to amuse himself, purchase a bookbag or small zippered travel bag for each child before you leave home. A decorated large paper bag can do just as well although it can tip and spill more easily. Into this bag put pencils, markers, crayons, writing paper, coloring books, workbooks, word games, crossword puzzle books, and small toys such as stuffed animals, finger puppets, miniature cars and trucks, and so forth. A clipboard serves to make writing easier. Add a generous assortment of paperback picture books and novels appropriate to the age of your child. The secret to success in the use of this bookbag lies in limiting its use to times when you are traveling in the car. Don't let the kids take the bag out at home because then there will be no novelty to the contents. If the trip is especially long, or if your child is very young, don't put all the items into the bag at the start of the trip. Gift wrap some for a surprise at breakfast each day.

If you own a small cassette tape recorder, bring that along with plenty of spare batteries. Before leaving home, record children's songs and stories from records in the library. You may have to schedule time each day for each child to use the recorder so there is no bickering over whose turn it is. Bring along a set of earphones, so everyone doesn't have to listen all the time.

Out-of-state license-plate counting is an activity that seems to fascinate all kids. Make some outline maps of the country by tracing a United States map from an atlas. Better yet, let the kids do this ahead of time. Then when a license plate is spotted the child puts a mark in the appropriate state. You can keep one map for the entire trip or begin a new one each day. As an extra bonus, your child will learn a lot of geography while amusing himself.

There are a lot of ways to spend the family times. You can take along a few songbooks and sing together. There are also numerous word games and alphabet games that are fun. Borrow a book of such games from the library ahead of time and make a list that you and the kids can choose from. Discuss the past day's events and what you expect to see at the next stop.

Be aware of the physical needs of children traveling. Their bodies need to move. Since movement in the car is necessarily limited, stop once each hour and encourage the kids to exercise or run if there's a safe place to do so. A few screams or yells will also help them to let off steam. The more active the stops, the better. Roadside rest areas are good for these stops because there's usually space to be very active. If you have a station wagon, buy a piece of foam, so the kids can occasionally lie down in the back.

Plan snack times rather than letting kids eat continuously in the car. Kids then have something to anticipate. If you are traveling on a major highway you can plan to serve a snack after you pass a certain exit. Then the kids will have fun watching for this exit.

Now for the squabbles between kids. To eliminate arguments over who sits where, make a seating schedule together before you leave and tape it to the back of the front seat. Schedule frequent switches. Include the parent who isn't driving in the switches—there is no law that says adults must always sit in the front!

If the kids squabble over anything else while you are driving, don't try to settle the problems for them. Just pull off the road, stop the car and busy yourself with a book or magazine. Say only that you will drive again when all is peaceful. The kids will learn quickly after one or two such stops that squabbling simply is not permitted in a moving car.

Learn While Traveling

Q. We plan to take many trips this vacation with our children. Are there ways we can involve our children in these trips that will strengthen the academic skills they've learned in school?

A. Summer trips offer many opportunities for children to learn and practice school-related skills. With careful planning you can incorporate reading, writing, mathematics, history, and geography into your travel plans.

Begin before the trip gets under way by inviting your children to join you in activities that will increase their knowledge of the area to which they will be going. Visit a local travel agency, public library, and automobile agency such as AAA for information and guidebooks on the area. At the library you can also look through the yellow pages of the phone book for the area; these pages are gold mines containing all kinds of information. Besides restaurants and motels, you can look up museums, parks, historical societies, information agencies, and so forth. If time allows, encourage your children to write to the local Chambers of Commerce for visitor information.

Study the atlas together. Use the atlas for route information and calculate the mileage, using alternative routes to an area. Look at any specialty charts that the atlas may contain for information on vegetation, land forms and land usage, population density, precipitation, industry, and so on. Your kids will learn good map-reading skills while accumulating valuable information on the area you'll visit.

Develop your kids' money management skills by providing little notebooks in which they can keep records of any money they spend. Some parents give a child a set amount of money to spend for the entire trip and let the child budget the money and decide how it is to be spent. For a younger child, give a small amount of money per day or per major stop. Let the spending decision be the child's. Your older kids will practice good math skills figuring out what they can afford and what they can't. They might even learn to save a bit one day to buy something else the next.

Older children can keep the expense records for the family, including gasoline and other transportation costs, food, motels, and so on. Let them keep track of the mileage and gasoline and calculate the miles per gallon for your car. They will be surprised at the costs of everything and might just develop a realistic view of the value of the dollar.

Let the children actually handle cash transactions, paying for food, gas, and so forth. This gives valuable experience using money and making change.

Allow the family to experience the local color of an area by leaving the superhighways for an hour a day and traveling the local state road that often parallels the highway. Increase your child's interest in history by stopping to read historical markers along the way. Visit local stores if they seem very different from stores back home. Buy a local newspaper; save the paper so you can compare the papers from different cities along the way.

Traveling affords much opportunity to practice writing skills. Notebooks for your children can be used to keep daily journals. Encourage photography. Later, when the pictures are developed, the kids can make books of their trip by pasting one picture on a sheet of blank paper and then, using their journal for information, writing a few sentences about where they were when the picture was taken and what was happening.

Letters and postcards sent to friends and relatives will also provide chances to practice writing skills. Prepare a list of addresses in advance.

Summer Reading Activities

Q. What are some ways I can motivate my children to read a lot this summer?

A. Your local library can help you encourage your children to read this summer. In many communities the library offers summer reading clubs for youngsters of all ages. Plan weekly family outings to the library to gather and exchange books. While you are there with your children, explore together the different types of reading material available. The number and quality of magazines available for children has increased recently, and these magazines are very popular. Explore the library's nonfiction section together. Show your children where they can find books about their hobbies or about any summer project they are interested in. Many kids get hooked on books by reading one book in a series; then they want to read all the rest. Ask your librarian to point out these series. Also ask the librarian for help in finding high interest, low vocabulary books for the reluctant reader.

Some children are motivated to read more if they see a visual representation of what they have read. You can simply keep a list of books read on file cards. Or you can make a bookworm out of colored paper and add a segment to the worm with the name of each book read. Or make a book tree:

place a small twig in a coffee can filled with dirt and hang pieces of paper from the twig with the names of books read.

Schedule a book discussion time once a week at dinner. Let each person discuss his reading for the week. Ask questions about the characters, the action, the illustrations in the book. Your child will develop good verbal skills during such discussions.

Stay involved in reading activities yourself. Keep books and magazines that you read in conspicuous places and read frequently in front of the kids so they can see your example. Have older kids read to younger ones while you listen. Select a book to be read aloud to the entire family, especially a book that is of interest to the kids but a bit too difficult for them to read by themselves.

You needn't get involved in the mechanics of reading over the summer; the kids get plenty of direct instruction from their teachers ten months of the year. However, words are the building blocks of reading and if your child develops facility with words he will be a better reader. Use lazy times in the summer, perhaps when traveling or hiking together, to play word games. Any games you make up that have to do with opposites, or synonyms (words that mean the same thing), or homonyms (words that sound alike but are spelled differently) are good. Play word category games, finding as many words as you can that describe shapes, for example, or all the words for warm weather clothing. Use unfamiliar words with the kids and make a game out of learning new vocabulary.

For the beginning reader in your house, do what teachers call language experience activities. Have your child tell a story or recount an outing the family had or a recent event. Write down what the child says. Allow the child to illustrate the story if he desires. Then read this story to the child frequently or let him read it himself if he can. Reading his own words is a powerful motivation for the younger child toward learning to read.

Points to Remember

It's important for children to learn to entertain themselves. A parent is not a twenty-four-hour-a-day recreation director.

Rules and routines are essential during vacations.

Vacation from school does not mean vacation from family and household responsibilities.

Plan ahead, with the kids' help, to make vacation trips a time of pleasant learning experiences.

Use vacation days to encourage your children to read for pleasure.

12

Common Childhood Concerns

Each of the previous chapters in this book has dealt with a specific category of parental concerns such as clothes, money, vacations, and so forth. This last chapter is different. The problems described in each of the questions aren't necessarily related to each other by topic, yet each question represents a concern or problem that most parents face sooner or later with one or more of their children.

Often parents ask me if there's a way to avoid ever having some of these problems. Their hope is that somehow, if they are good enough parents and do enough of the right things, if they shower their kids with enough love, they will avoid some of these common childhood concerns.

It's unreasonable, no matter how good a parent you are, to think you can escape having to cope with problems as the children grow. Behaviors that seem perfectly okay to the kids

will not seem okay to you. When a group of people live together closely as a family it's inevitable that needs will clash,
emotions will flare, and disagreements will arise.

Because the situations that follow occur in so many
families today, they are accepted as "normal," as problems
that must be lived with until the kids somehow outgrow them.
Nothing could be further from the truth. The fact that these
problems arise with great frequency is not enough reason to
view them as insoluble.

Before you grapple with some of these problems, take a
moment to review some of the hints for applying new skills and
techniques that you learned in Chapter 2. Remember to work
on solving only one problem at a time, and not to tackle the
hardest problem first. The older your children are, the more
important it is for you to share the strategy with them, to
discuss the problems and proposed solutions together. Utilize
the brainstorming technique described on P. 75 to devise a
variety of possible solutions. Use only the language of respect
with children of all ages. Give appropriate choices, and allow
agreed upon consequences to occur, even if these consequences mean temporary discomfort and unhappiness for
your child. Expect improvement, not perfection, both in the
behavior of the children and in your ability to cope with them.

Winning over Whining

Q. How can I stop my six-year-old daughter from whining?

A. It's much easier to stop a parent from listening than to
stop a child from whining. The end result will be the same—
you won't hear any whining.

Kids sometimes whine because it is a very effective way of
getting undue attention from their parents. Other times they
whine in order to get their own way. Kids learn at a very young
age that if they whine long enough many parents will give in

Encourage Yourself As you read all of the problems described in this book, keep a cumulative list of all the problems you *don't* have. It's so easy to feel overwhelmed when things do not go smoothly that parents often lose their perspective and forget just how many potential problem areas they have managed to avoid. Feel encouraged that you had the wisdom to avoid so many other potential problems.

just to stop the noise. This method of manipulating parents succeeds just often enough to reinforce the whining behavior.

So let's talk about how a parent can stop listening. Maybe you are the kind of parent who can just decide not to hear; if so, tell your daughter only once that she has the choice whether or not she wishes to continue to whine, but that you have decided that you'll listen no longer.

Some parents find that even when they decide not to listen they just cannot tune out their kid's whining. So here are some hints to make not listening a bit easier. Vanishing is an effective parenting technique. When your daughter starts to whine, go to a place in the house where you can't hear her. Dr. Dreikurs, in his book *Children: The Challenge,* recommends the use of the bathroom as a refuge for the vanishing parent. Sometimes the bathroom is the only place in the house where a child won't follow. Stock your bathroom with a small radio and some magazines so you can enjoy your vanishing moments.

Another help in tuning out a whining kid is to wear a pair of big fluffy earmuffs. That will give the child a strong visual signal that her behavior is unacceptable.

Another option is to enlist your daughter's help in changing inappropriate family behavior. The parent counterpart to children's whining is yelling. Kids hate it when an adult yells at them and often display uncooperative behavior toward the parents as a result. In addition to the fact that yelling causes resentment in kids, it is an ineffective parenting technique simply because it does not bring about the desired behavior change on a permanent basis. If it did, we'd have no more misbehaving kids, because if there is one skill many parents know and use consistently, it's yelling. So, buy two pairs of earmuffs. Ask your daughter to help you change your inappropriate behavior by putting on her earmuffs and not listening when you yell. Tell her you will do the same when she whines. Perhaps your spouse would like a pair of earmuffs too.

Yelling When I talk with children, I find the parental behavior they complain about most is yelling. Yelling is seen by the kids as an unfair, heavy-handed device of parental domination. Sometimes the kids will comply with whatever it is the parent is yelling about, sometimes not. In either case, the yelling sparks unpleasant feelings in the child toward the parent. These feelings often are translated into revenge behaviors at some later date, behaviors that the kid uses to get even with the parents. So, while yelling might accomplish a parent's immediate goals, the side effects of unpleasant feelings and the possibility of future revenge behaviors make yelling a technique most parents would do better to avoid.

Taming Temper Tantrums

Q. I have two kids who love to scream or throw temper tantrums when they get angry about something. How can I put a stop to this behavior?

A. Screams and temper tantrums are social behaviors, meant to have an audience. Did you ever know a child who went in to his room, closed the door, and then screamed or had the tantrum? More likely, you're familiar with kids who display these behaviors right under your feet. When you attempt to escape the scene they follow, all the while continuing to scream and create a fuss.

To put a stop to this behavior, you need to stop being the audience, either physically or psychologically or both.

You can physically remove yourself more easily than you can an angry child. This is the time for the bathroom technique. Pretend that nature has called, disappear into the bathroom, turn on a radio or read a magazine that you keep handy in the bathroom for just such times, and relax until the storm passes. A move to any other area in the house where the child can't follow will work just as well.

You can remove yourself psychologically by remaining where you are and demonstrating to the child that you are not affected by screams and tantrums. Just continue whatever you were doing when the storm broke. You can use a bright, conspicuous pair of earmuffs to demonstrate visually that you are not listening.

One resourceful father, when he senses a temper tantrum about to erupt, gets his pipe, relaxes in his favorite chair, and announces in a calm, matter-of-fact voice, "OK, son, I have plenty of time now, let's have the temper tantrum."

Terminate Tattling

Q. I'm tired of listening to my children tattle on each other. I have read that parents should always listen to what kids have on their minds but I really hate listening to all the stories they tell about each other. How can I get them to stop?

A. It's appropriate to listen to what kids have to say about themselves and their own feelings, but not what they have to say about what someone else is doing. The best way to get them to stop is to refuse to listen. Retreat to your bedroom or the bathroom if that is the only way you can not listen. It is important not to get involved with the tattler.

The child who tattles is really saying "Look at what I'm not doing." It is an attempt to make the sibling look bad in comparison to the tattler and to bring down the wrath of Mom or Dad on the other person. Kids must learn to solve difficulties in their relationships by themselves. They can only do this if parents refuse to interfere.

Ignore the Interrupter

Q. What can I do with kids who constantly interrupt my conversations? I can't say two words to anyone, even my wife, without my kids interrupting to ask a question or tell me something. I've told them a hundred times to wait until I'm finished talking but they still interrupt. What else can I try?

A. This is the time to ignore the precept "always listen to your kids." Don't listen to them while you are having a conversation with someone else. It is disrespectful to the other person and to yourself as well to let an interrupting kid monopolize your conversation.

Explain to the kids that when you are talking to someone else you will not allow yourself to be interrupted, that you will not acknowledge them verbally but will instead continue your conversation.

You can acknowledge a child's presence physically with a hand on his shoulder or around his waist, but do not talk to him until your conversation is at a natural breaking point. If he continues to interrupt, say nothing more to him but simply move to another room and continue the conversation. In an extreme case you might have to move behind a locked door. Once the children see that you mean it when you say you refuse to be interrupted, you won't have to move your conversations elsewhere.

Some role-playing around this issue would be fun and informative for the whole family. The younger the children are, the more important it is actually to walk them through the paces of the new situation. To role-play, tell the kids you are going to have a rehearsal of how to act when one person is talking with another person. Have two family members stage a conversation and have another interrupt. The original two continue their conversation, following the steps mentioned previously. Be sure in role-playing that everyone gets a chance to play the different roles. Afterward, be sure to discuss how it felt in each of the roles.

Coping with Curses

Q. My son has been learning a lot of four-letter words at school. I have repeatedly told him that such words are not allowed in our house. Yet he continues to use them, even though he knows it upsets me. His grandmother absolutely turned purple when she heard him use such words! When I was young, parents used to wash out their kids' mouths with soap for using dirty language. Do you think this kind of punishment will make a kid stop today?

A. You have correctly guessed the reason for your son's behavior—it shocks and upsets adults, and focuses a lot of attention on him. What a powerful force, right in his own mouth where no one can stop him from using it. Whenever he's mad at you, he can take revenge by displaying, usually in front of grandparents or company, his accomplished vocabulary.

It would certainly be simple if cleaning the inside of a child's mouth would also clean up his vocabulary. For a few kids, this does work. For many more, the chance to shock and upset the adults is worth an occasional mouth washing. Remember, he is expecting you to be very upset, that's what he wants. So if you oblige, by ranting and raging and telling him how bad he is while washing out his mouth, you have actually rewarded him for his unacceptable behavior.

It's often much more effective to give an unexpected reaction when a child uses four-letter words. This way you take away the power of his words and defuse the situation.

There are three useful responses you can choose from. All have worked for many, many parents.

The first is simply to ignore the words completely. Don't respond at all. Don't correct, criticize, lecture, or threaten. Just go on doing whatever it is you were doing. Respond to him as if the words hadn't been said. What will happen, of course, is that he will be surprised and disbelieving. He'll actually use the words more frequently for a while. He might even fish for a reaction, saying "Didn't you hear me, Ma?" Keep ignoring, and finally he'll learn that using four-letter words in the family is pointless. Nobody listens!

A second unexpected reaction is to play dumb, to pretend you don't know what the word means. "What did you say, Billy? I'm not sure what ____ means. Would you please explain it to me?"

A third unexpected reaction is to seize the moment and use it for a short, simple lesson in sex education and family living. Say to him "I see you have learned the word ____. Did you know it means _____?" Give a simple, one sentence, straightforward explanation of the word. Then add, "Sometimes people use this word when they are angry and when they want to upset and hurt someone else. If you are angry at me, come and tell me, and we'll talk about it. We don't need these words to express anger."

Cool It in the Car

Q. I'm always a nervous wreck when I get behind the wheel of a car. My kids fight, cry, complain, and horse around. I find my attention divided between them and the road. Someday I'm afraid we're going to have a serious accident because of this. How can I get my children to stop fighting in the car?

A. Pull off the road at the first opportunity. Tell the children in a calm, friendly voice that you find it impossible to drive safely when there is fighting in the car and that you have decided to just sit and wait until everyone decides to quiet down. Say nothing more. You need not explain why it is unsafe; the children will undoubtedly determine who started the fight, who is in the right. The children can and will settle their own disagreements if adults do not take that job upon themselves. It may take a short while for the children to understand that Mom or Dad is serious and really does not intend to drive unless they settle down. Every time thereafter when the children are disruptive in the car, stop, say nothing, and wait. The fighting will diminish.

Bewildered by Bedwetting

Q. We have an eleven-year-old son who still wets the bed on most nights. Our pediatrician can find nothing physically wrong with him. We have tried punishing him by not letting him watch TV on days when his bed is wet in the morning. That didn't work. Then we tried rewarding him with a dime every night he remained dry. That didn't work either. Do you know of anything else we can try?

A. Bedwetting among older children occurs more frequently than most people realize. You did the right thing by checking with your physician first, although rarely is it found that bedwetting stems from a physical cause.

An understanding of some of the psychological dynamics involved in bedwetting will help you deal with the problem more effectively. Bedwetting is an effective tool for the child to get lots of special attention and service. For some children it is a powerful means of showing the parents that the child is boss and that the parents cannot control the child's "water power." For other children, bedwetting is a way to get even with parents for other problems in the parent/child relationship.

The solution involves withdrawing the above psychological payoffs for the child and the use of logical consequences.

To avoid the payoffs, realize that bedwetting is the child's problem not the parents' problem. Refuse to become involved with the problem or to give the child extra service by changing the bed for him. Explain to your son in a friendly manner that he is eleven years old now and that you have great confidence in his ability to handle his bedwetting without help from Mom or Dad. Show him where clean linens are kept. Teach him how to strip his bed, how to put the wet linens through the washer and dryer, and how to put dry linens on the bed. Do not remind or nag him to change the bed once you have shown him how. The discomfort of a wet, smelly bed will be enough of a reminder.

Once you have taught him how to take care of his needs politely refuse to become involved further. No blaming, no criticizing, no humiliating him for his problem. Do not ask him how he is doing, or show delight when he is dry or discouragement if he wets. If he brings up the subject, ask him to express *his* feelings on how *he* is handling the bedwetting and express your confidence in his ability to take care of the problem. It may take a week, a month, a year, or even longer for the problem to disappear completely for your son. For you, the problem disappears the day you decide to let your son handle his own needs.

Turn off the Water Power

Q. My five-year-old child has frequent "accidents" because he just can't manage to get to the bathroom on time. I often remind him to stop playing as soon as he feels the urge to go, but he refuses to listen. I warn him that the other kids will make fun of him. I have nagged, scolded, and threatened, all to no avail. What next?

A. He has one thing stronger than all the nagging and threatening in the world—water power! You cannot control your child's bladder by force. Instead, change your response to these accidents so it is the child—not you—who experiences the consequences.

Explain to your son that he is old enough to decide whether he wishes to wet his pants or to use the bathroom. Tell him that he is able to dry himself and change his clothes without your help, so there is no reason for you to get involved.

Keep handy all the items your son needs to care for himself when he is wet. Include powder or cream if his skin often becomes sore and place a pail nearby for the wet clothes. Put these toiletries in the bathroom within his reach. Show him how to use these items in a helpful, friendly way. Let him see that this change in routine is happening out of your respect for his ability to care for his own needs, not out of your anger and frustration.

If the accidents occur frequently at school, allow him to take a bag to school that contains a washcloth, powder or cream, dry pants, and a plastic bag for the wet clothes. This allows him to take care of his own needs at school as well as at home.

Fighting in the Family

Q. There is no peace in our house. We have four children, ages seven, ten, thirteen, and fifteen. It's mainly the two children in the middle, both boys, who disrupt the entire household with their endless fighting and bickering. My husband and I were able to tolerate the fighting when they were smaller. We constantly explained to them how wrong it was to argue with each other, and frequently we punished them. We figured they would outgrow this behavior sooner or later. Well now it's later and the fighting is no better. I feel defeated in my efforts to provide a happy home for our family and resentful toward the boys. Is there anything you can think of that I haven't already done to end the fighting?

A. Any two people who live together must learn to settle differences between them. Perhaps you have friends who proudly say they never fight or disagree. This probably means they never really communicate honestly with each other either, and that potential conflict situations are invariably avoided by one person giving in. This avoidance of disagreement is not nearly as healthy as an honest airing of differences and a genuine attempt at solving the problems.

Conflicts between brothers and sisters are inevitable. Learning to deal with these conflicts is an essential part of growing up and preparing for independence. Parents who try to suppress the real issues between siblings and to establish "peace at any price" deny their children the opportunity to grow in this way.

To allow your children the opportunity to learn to solve their own problems you must learn to stay out of their fights completely. Staying out means not listening, not arbitrating, not judging, not threatening, not punishing. It especially means not lecturing the older child on how he should be able to stop the fights merely because he is older. The younger kids in the family are excellent at manipulating the older brothers and sisters into fights and then enjoying their parents' protection because they are the smaller.

Staying out of fights serves another purpose. Often kids fight because fighting is an effective way to get their parents' attention, not because there is a real issue to be resolved. By fighting, kids can also show the parents how powerful they are, since no matter what the parents do the fighting continues. When you take the parental audience away you take away the payoff for a lot of the arguing and bickering that goes on.

How can you stay out of the fights when the noise drives you crazy? Disappear into another room. Take a warm bath. Read a good book. Take a walk. Realize you are not giving in to your kids when you leave a certain area of the house because they are misbehaving. You are using temporary disappearance as a discipline technique that is very effective when the purpose of the kids' misbehavior is to involve the parent. Eventually you will find that you can stop hearing the bickering and can stop becoming involved even if it occurs in the same room with you. Then you'll no longer have to disappear physically. Although the fighting might not stop completely, you will find that peace in your family does not have to be shattered every time two members have a disagreement.

Stay out of the Fight

Q. I have trouble understanding why you advise parents to withdraw and stay out of it when their children fight and are disruptive. It seems to me it is a parent's job to *make* their kids stop fighting and cooperate.

A. If you have found a way to *make* kids stop fighting and being disruptive, please write and tell me what it is! Most parents who write tell me they have tried everything: lecturing, yelling, threatening, scolding, spanking, rewarding, punishing, and still the kids are at it.

All of the above behaviors that parents so frequently use have one main drawback. Since the parents focus on the children when they are disruptive, the kids actually receive attention for misbehavior. The kids have learned how to keep Mom and Dad busy with them by being disruptive. Many parents make the mistake of paying extra attention to the kids when they are misbehaving.

By staying out of fights the parent is withholding the payoffs that maintain the unwanted behavior. In that context, withdrawal is actually a positive, powerful, and effective parenting technique.

No Fighting at the Table

Q. I have tried your advice on staying out of children's fights. This has worked well for me except at mealtime. When the kids squabble during breakfast or dinner, I find myself annoyed and upset and unable to eat. The kids don't seem to mind the fights, but I do! Any other suggestions for squabbling at mealtime?

A. Yes. Instead of trying to ignore a fight going on at the table while you eat, you can use parental withdrawal or removal of the squabblers instead. Either technique is effective.

It is easier for the parents to withdraw when kids fight at mealtime. All this requires is that you take your plates of food and go into another room. Depending on where you normally eat, the kitchen or living room or even the bedroom is appropriate. You can go anywhere as long as you no longer have to have the fighting right under your nose. The nice feature of this technique is that it requires only the cooperation of the adults. It's effective in changing the kids' fighting behavior because you have denied them an audience, the main purpose for their fights. The message they get is "Your behavior is unacceptable. We refuse to eat with you while it continues." The kids will hear this message more clearly through your action of withdrawal than through lectures or words that tell them not to fight.

If you decide, instead, to remove the squabblers, you must do it in such a way that they can choose to stop fighting at any time. They must see clearly that you are not punishing them, that they are the ones who are choosing by their behavior to leave. Say to them, "You can either stay at the table and eat in peace or you may leave and continue the fight in your rooms. You decide." If they continue to fight, say, "I see you have chosen to go to your room. You're excused from the table." If they remain seated after they have been excused from the table, say, "Would you like to go to your rooms by yourself or would you like my help in getting there? You decide." It is important for them to see that you cannot be manipulated, that you will not allow them to eat at the table and fight with each other at the same time.

Once the kids experience the consequences of their mealtime fighting through your use of either of these methods, their mealtime behaviors should improve.

Plan Television Watching

Q. How can I get my children to watch less television?

A. This is a problem that plagues many parents. Children will often choose to sit glued to the tube by the hour. When parents shut off the set and tell the kids to do something else, an unpleasant confrontation often follows.

First, it is important to realize that TV is not an inherently horrible monster. Through watching high quality TV shows, kids can be exposed to the lands and peoples of the world, the wonders of science, the beauties of the arts. The challenge for parents is to guide children in recognizing and choosing the programs of value.

Influencing the children's TV choices takes time and planning on the parents' part. Sit down with the children when the weekly schedule appears in the newspaper and together make a family viewing schedule. This is the time for everyone to say which shows are valued and why. The final schedule will include choices made by both the parents and the children.

Post the schedule near the TV for the week. If a child asks to watch at a time not agreed upon, he can be reminded that the program is not on the list so the TV cannot be turned on. Children will accept a no from a list without getting into the power struggle that often occurs when it is the parent who says no.

After the children have watched a show it is helpful to take the time to discuss the content and merits of the program with them. This type of discussion will strengthen a child's verbal and analytical skills in addition to guiding future TV choices.

Feet on the Floor

Q. We live in a small apartment and our TV set is in the living room. The room is nicely furnished, though the couch and chairs are not expensive. The problem is that our kids put their feet on the furniture and sometimes even roughhouse and jump on the couch. We have yelled at them and even spanked them, but this never stops them for long. How can I get them to stop for good?

A. They will stop mistreating the furniture as soon as you stop talking and yelling about it and take more effective action. Your letter illustrates how ineffective "parent talk" usually is. So what if Mom and Dad yell at us or even lightly swat our bottoms. We can outlast them and keep right on doing what we were doing.

So change from words to action. Calmly give the kids the choice of treating the furniture appropriately or leaving the living room. Appropriately means no feet on the furniture, no standing or jumping on couches or chairs. Be sure the kids are clear about which behaviors are appropriate.

If they stop when given this choice, fine, say no more. If they continue, say, "I see you have chosen to leave the room." Turn off the TV without a word, ignore their protests and escort them to another room.

If they balk, give them another choice: "You may go by yourself or I will take you." Tell them they may return in ten minutes if they will then choose to treat the furniture appropriately. If their behavior continues to be inappropriate when they return, give them the same choice but increase the amount of time before they can return.

By acting instead of talking you are providing an effective consequence to the kids' behavior. Treat the furniture correctly and you can stay in the living room and watch TV; mistreat the furniture and the TV goes off and you leave the room. The choice is up to the kids.

Don't Try to Nip Nail-Biting

Q. My daughter is ten and she bites her nails. She does this only when she is with kids her own age, at school. My husband and I have tried everything. How do we build her confidence in herself so that she will stop?

A. When coping with a persistent habit such as nail-biting, it is more effective to remain uninvolved with the problem than to actively try to change the child's behavior.

The reason that doing less accomplishes more is that the child may perceive parental involvement as personally beneficial. I once counseled a twelve-year-old boy with a nail-biting problem. He described to me the frequent long talks his parents had with him about the problem, how they outlined all the negative effects of nail-biting, and how they offered him all kinds of rewards to stop. The boy enjoyed these talks immensely! The talks provided much extra involvement and attention from his parents. It certainly was worth it to him to keep the nail-biting habit when it led to this constant show of parental concern.

The moral of this story is that all the special attention parents pay to such a problem actually reinforces the behavior.

Nail-biting is a problem that belongs to the child, not the parent. Ask yourself what would be the worst thing that could happen if your child never gave up this habit. Unsightly hands, perhaps, but that's about all. Don't read any deep psychological significance into the habit. There's no proof that biting nails means the child feels unloved, un-self-confident, or inadequate.

My recommendation to you is to do the one thing you and your husband have not yet tried—stay uninvolved. No nagging, reminding, or scolding, no asking to see her nails to check whether she is still biting them. Build your child's self-confidence by expressing your belief in her ability to solve *her* problem with nail-biting however and whenever *she* decides to do so.

The Old Piano-Practice Blues

Q. My daughter has been taking piano lessons for more than a year now and I'm not sure I can stand our fights over practicing much longer. I find myself constantly nagging her to practice her music. She tells me she will do it soon, then she dawdles and puts it off until it is almost bedtime. That's when I start yelling. She ends up in tears, declaring she wants to quit. How can I make her practice the piano without all this hassle?

A. The key to the conflict is found in your words, *make her practice.* You have turned the experience of learning to play an instrument, which should be enjoyable, into an unpleasant

---

Parental Fantasies We set up ourselves and our children for a great deal of disappointment when we create fantasies about our children's futures according to our own expectations and desires. The children become disappointed because the parental expectations are often unrealistic and impossible to meet. The parents become disappointed because they feel they have given and sacrificed much for the sake of their kids and not got what they expected to get in return.

There are several common parental fantasies. Many of us want our kids to be all that we aren't. A short father might want a tall son. The quiet, socially shy parents might want their child to be easygoing and talkative. An unhappy mother might want her children to live happy, romantic lives. We often expect our kids to do and accomplish what we haven't. They'll go to college, play football, have a high-paying job, and experience the personal and professional success that passed us by.

Our children are not an extension of us and our own hopes and dreams. They have their own goals and must grow and mature in their own fashion. Parents will escape disappointment and reap much joy when they give up their parental fantasies for their children and instead delight in watching their kids fulfill their own dreams and potentials.

battle of wills. She is resisting not the piano, per se, but your efforts to boss and control her.

To solve this problem you must first look at the situation objectively to determine whether taking lessons is your decision or your child's. If your child does not want lessons in the first place, she is not likely to practice on her own under any circumstances. If this is the case, perhaps you should stop the lessons.

If your child really does want to learn, then the solution lies in giving her some legitimate choices within a framework guided by you and the music teacher. First, sit down with your daughter and her teacher and find out just how much practicing is recommended. Then list the options for meeting these requirements. The longer the list of options, the greater the chance of a successful solution. For example, if the teacher suggests thirty-minute practice sessions five times a week, let your daughter choose which days and times she wants to practice. Post the schedule she writes out over the piano. If the teacher says only how many minutes per week of practicing is recommended, your daughter could decide how she would like to break this time down. Again, post the schedule she makes. Once the option to be used is chosen, you must agree not to nag or remind her to practice.

Anytime you try to use force with a child you run the risk of resentment and resistance. When, instead, you offer a limited choice of options, you build mutual respect and trust.

Fostering Friendships

Q. I have a daughter who is a loner, both at home and at school. Teachers have often told me that she has few friends at school, sits by herself in the cafeteria, and doesn't like to go out on the playground at lunch time. At home she'd much rather read or watch TV than go outside and play with the neighborhood kids. Should I just accept the fact that she's a loner and leave her alone, or is there something I can do to help her become more outgoing?

A. Accept the fact that some children naturally seem to be more outgoing than others. Some like to hang around with a crowd, others prefer to stick with one or two close friends. Don't put constant pressure on your daughter to change; the more you do, the more she'll resist your efforts. Be careful not to use the labels *loner* or *shy* in her presence, for they will only reinforce the behaviors you would like to change.

You can, however, help her form some friendships without using pressure. Invite another family with a daughter her age to share activities with your family. Perhaps a joint supper or a movie or an evening of monopoly would be fun. Make your yard an inviting place for neighborhood children to come to play. Some children feel okay about playing with others as long as they are close to home. Encourage her to join any activity groups in which she shows interest, particularly if the activity is a noncompetitive one. Swimming, gymnastics, ballet, scouts, library book clubs are all possibilities. Friendships can grow from shared interests and activities.

The school is in an even better position to help your child form friendships. Visit her school and talk with all of her teachers. The object of your visit is to make the teachers more aware of who your child is, especially her strengths, special interests, and any unusual and exciting experiences she has had. Teachers are so busy that frequently they don't take the time to look behind the quiet exterior of a shy child. When they know your child better, teachers can devise ways to help foster friendships. One way might be to organize a special interest group that studies a subject and makes a presentation to the class. Another might be to pair your daughter with another child who needs extra help in a subject that your daughter knows well. Some schools organize special activity groups at lunch time to mix kids who are usually alone with others who are outgoing.

It's not enough for the school to report to you that your daughter is a loner. Specific plans need to be made to encourage her to join in more with the other children. You can help by providing the information her teachers need to get to know your daughter as a complete person, not just a face in the crowd.

Where Did I Come From?

Q. I have three children ranging in age from five to eleven. Whenever they ask questions about babies and sexual stuff I get uncomfortable and don't know what to say. Their dad is just as uncomfortable with this subject as I am. Don't all schools have sex education programs so that parents don't really have to answer these questions?

A. It is very important for parents to explain the facts of life to their children. Less than ten percent of American schools have comprehensive sex education programs. Even those schools that do have such programs insist that their role is simply supplementary, that parents are the primary sex educators of their children. Schools usually provide only information. It is up to the parents to convey values, standards, and attitudes.

Many parents are uncomfortable about explaining the facts of life to their children because they don't know how much to tell their kids. To avoid this problem, first ask the kids what they already know about the specific subject before you answer their questions. That will give you an idea about what they do know and how accurate their information is. Then answer the question asked as honestly as you can using correct terminology for body parts and functions. Avoid slang terms. Give as much information as you feel the children have asked for. You don't have to tell them all the facts of life the first time the subject comes up. If they want more information, they'll ask. On the other hand, there really is little danger of telling too much, as many parents fear. If you offer young children more information than they want, or information that is too advanced, the children will stop listening and most likely will change the subject or walk away.

Don't let your feelings of discomfort stop you from having frank talks with your children. It's okay if you are not perfectly at ease and hesitate a bit to decide how you want to phrase things. The important thing is to let your children know it's okay to be curious and to want to know the facts of life. Let them know that they can come to you anytime they have a question or concern; because if your kids don't feel it is okay to ask you, they'll probably ask a friend and end up with a lot of unhelpful misinformation.

Doctor in Disguise

Q. This was bound to happen sooner or later because my six-year-old son usually plays with the little girl next door after school. Yesterday, while I was sitting in the kitchen having coffee with her mother, we noticed the kids were unusually quiet. We went to see what was happening and found my son with his pants off, undergoing a make-believe "operation" performed by his friend the "doctor." We were speechless! We know all kids sooner or later play doctor but didn't have any idea how to react. We distracted them by telling them to come for cookies and milk. What else should we do?

A. I'm glad you reacted so calmly, for some parents become extremely upset and react with anger when confronted with young kids playing doctor. It is not a time to react harshly or punitively. Children are naturally curious about their own bodies and the bodies of others of both the same and the opposite sex. Exploration through doctor games as a way to satisfy that curiosity comes just as naturally. You do not need to scare them so they never do such a thing again.

This is an ideal time to teach your son about public and private parts of the body. Explain calmly to him that we all have some parts of our bodies, our genitals, that are considered private and are not to be displayed in public. Playing doctor is okay as long as these private parts are covered up, not exposed, and not touched by others. Explain that a real doctor may have to examine these parts, and that is appropriate, but it is inappropriate to show these private parts to friends. Use the words *appropriate* and *inappropriate* instead of *good* and *bad* so your child doesn't learn to associate private parts of his body with bad or guilty feelings.

Self-Sufficient Scouts

Q. Our daughter is a girl scout and likes to earn badges. Sometimes I think it's her father and I who should receive the badges, not her! She asks us for an awful lot of help in completing the assignments. She finds it difficult to organize things and almost never cleans up after working on a scout project. Just how much help should a parent give to a scout trying to earn a badge?

A. We rob our children of many chances to grow and mature by doing too much for them. It is all too easy for an experienced parent to organize things for a child, which keeps the child from learning to do this for herself. Remember, a good self-concept is based on self-reliance and the knowledge that

---

Immediate Responses It isn't always easy to instantaneously come up with the best solution to a child's misbehavior. When we react too quickly to a situation, we often regret the action we did take. Feel free to say to a child, "I need to think about this situation for a little while before I decide what is to be done." A well-thought-out solution, even if it comes after a short delay, is usually more effective than an action taken in haste and anger.

one can do for oneself what needs to be done. She'll learn to clean up if you don't do it for her. Establish a rule that the next activity cannot begin until the previous one is cleaned up.

Instead of helping by doing, help by encouraging. Listen to your daughter's plans as she works for her badges. Offer supportive statements such as "I know you can figure it out" when needed. Express delight in her accomplishments and celebrate with her when she receives a badge that she really has earned on her own.

Points to Remember

Search for effective solutions when a problem arises rather than giving up and just living with it.

Involve your kids when you search for solutions to problems. Be firm and consistent in your resolve to carry through on the solutions chosen.

Act instead of talking.

Change your response to a misbehavior rather than trying to somehow change the child.

Stay out of situations that the child must solve for himself.

Suggested Reading

Children: The Challenge, Dreikurs and Soltz, E. P. Dutton, 1964.

How to Raise an Independent Child, Gould, St. Martin's Press, 1979.

How to Stop Fighting with Your Kids, Dreikurs, Corsini, and Gould, Ace Books, 1974.

The Practical Parent, Corsini and Painter, Harper and Row, 1975.

Raising a Responsible Child, Dinkmeyer and McKay, Simon and Schuster, 1973.

Raising the Exceptional Child, Yura and Zuckerman, E. P. Dutton, 1979.

Redirecting Children's Misbehavior, Kvols-Reidler, R.D.I.C. Publications, Boulder, Colorado, 1979.

An Invitation

This book has been written in response to the many questions sent to me by parents searching for solutions to the problems of raising children. It is my hope that my answers to their questions will help you to cope more effectively with your own children.

Perhaps you have a concern that has not been discussed here. Or you may have a solution to some of the problems in the book that is different from mine, which you'd be willing to share. If so, I invite you to send your questions and solutions to me at P.O. 260421, Tampa, Florida, 33614.